Savage
Island

"Brian Moreland, an author well versed in folklore, myth, and history who infuses that knowledge into his writing and elevates it to a level above that which we normally see in horror fiction outside some of the masters like Rice, King, and Barker."

— iHorror.com

"Moreland combines the best of what I love about horror fiction, impeccable prose, characters with a life-like depth, fantastic monsters and a palpable sense of dread that seemingly lunges off the pages and grabs you by the throat."

— Peter Schwotzer, *Famous Monsters of Filmland*

"*Tomb of Gods* completely knocked me out from beginning to end, with some of the sequences so unrelentingly fast moving it was impossible to put down … In true Indiana Jones style, the hunt to find the tomb and decipher Riley's cryptic diary is on, with the baton being passed to Egyptologist Imogen Riley, who is Harlan's granddaughter…the mythology explored in the second half of the story is simply outstanding, expanding into unexpected supernatural and theological directions…an absolute delight."

— Tony's Top 10 Horror Novels of 2020, HorrorDNA.com

"What starts out as a good adventure story, grows into so much more as it moves along. *Tomb of Gods* is fantastically imaginative, darkly fun, and horrifically astounding; I expect this book to make my Top 10 Reads of 2020."

— Dead Head Reviews

"The suspense of the story, aided by sly hints from the author, and the atmosphere of a dark, claustrophobic tomb work together to create a scary story. The characters' fear invites the reader into the world to experience the fright themselves."

— Booklist Starred Review *for Tomb of Gods*

"Moreland's tale is nicely paced and laced with palpable tension… Horror fans will be pleased as the terrors of the tomb force each character to confront a past trauma."

— **Publishers Weekly**

"*The Devil's Woods* is a force of nature. A complex, chilling foray into the darkness of a forbidden land, and man's tortured soul."

— **Hunter Shea,** author of *Swamp Monster Massacre* and *Sinister Entity*

"*The Devil's Woods* is an awesome horror novel, filled with nerve-wracking suspense and thrilling action!"

— **Jeff Strand,** author of *Wolf Hunt*

"*Darkness Rising* is a bit *Hellraiser*, a bit *Romeo and Juliet* and a lot of signature Brian Moreland. It's wonderful."

— **Haddonfeld Horror**

"*Darkness Rising* is to imagine *The Crow*…then add a dash of H.P. Lovecraft and Clive Barker."

— **Ravenous Monster**

"I really enjoyed *Darkness Rising*… If you are a fan of Moreland or the genre, you owe it to yourself to add this to your collection."

—**Horror After Dark**

"Brian Moreland writes with one eye on characterisation and the other on scaring the life out of you."

— **Maynard Sims,** author of *Stronghold* and *The Eighth Witch*

Savage
Island

by
Brian Moreland

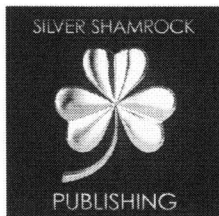

SILVER SHAMROCK

PUBLISHING

```
CW  |        CONTENT WARNINGS
    | This book may contain content that triggers undesired reactions.
    |              SEXUAL ASSAULT
```

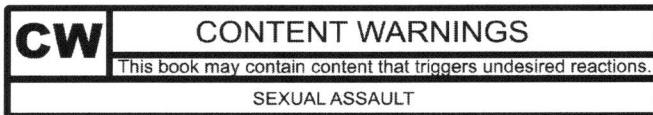

Copyright © 2021 Brian Moreland

Front Cover Design by Kealan Patrick Burke
Interior art by Bob Veon
Formatted by Kenneth W. Cain
Edited by Kenneth W. Cain

All rights reserved.

"With savages, the weak in body or mind are soon eliminated."
— Charles Darwin, *The Descent of Man*

PROLOGUE

Somewhere in the Philippine Islands

Hold me, Daddy. Those were the last words little Ellie had said to him before her final breath gave out, while cradled in his arms. That was the day Skipper Jim Walker's heart died, became a cold, unfeeling thing withered in his chest. Yet somehow he endured a few more weeks, thin as a walking scarecrow, clothes hanging on him in filthy tatters, but alive. During the savage days and nights that he'd been stranded on this godforsaken island, suffered through monsoons and sweltering heat, starvation and dehydration, his will to survive had gotten him through one day to the next.

Hold me, Daddy… His daughter's voice was a constant passenger in his mind. Her ghostly form walked through his dreams and reminded him of the mistake he'd made in coming here.

"I've got to get off this bloody island," Skipper Jim muttered.

"You've tried a thousand times already," he argued with himself. "It's no use."

"Another day," he pleaded. "Someone will rescue me." Even as he said it, he knew he was clinging to false hope. His radio was dead and no one back home in Sydney knew where to find him. *Lost at sea*, would be the conclusion of any searchers.

The part of him that was ready to give up said, "Quit prolonging the inevitable."

Skipper Jim nodded solemnly as he walked across the deck of his beached fishing boat. High winds rustled the surrounding palm trees and scattered dead fronds and coconut husks across the island. Gray clouds roiled overhead. The air filled with cool dampness that prickled his skin. Climbing down into the cramped quarters of the below decks, Skipper Jim battened down the hatches. He heard more than just the oncoming storm rustling outside. Something banged against the hull, like pounding fists of someone wanting to get in. More thuds sounded from the upper deck.

"Just the wind flinging debris and coconuts," he told himself.

He took a swig of whiskey to calm his nerves. His wounded hand stung down to the bone. Blood was seeping through the moss-stained bandage. He unraveled the cloth and examined the bite. Nasty teeth marks. Light green lichen that grew on everything outside now infested the rents in his left hand. He doused the wound with alcohol and then rewrapped it. With his good hand, he pulled out his skipper's log and began to write:

Day thirty-two: Marooned here for weeks now on some Philippine island. A boat passing by only sees thick mangroves that surround its perimeter, trees of a dark jungle, a few looming cliffs. On the west side, where mangroves offer an opening, a narrow passage leads into a lagoon. It was the beauty of this hidden paradise that lured us in. We cruised our fishing boat here on holiday to escape from the civilized world. We anchored near the lagoon's beach, picnicked, and swam.

Then we made the mistake of exploring the island. God, what a nightmare. I'm the only survivor.

Tears rolled down Jim's cheeks as he thought of his wife and daughter.

I've yelled at passing boats 'til my lungs hurt. I've expended my flares. Burned fires to attract the attention of far-off planes, yet no one comes. Perhaps it's best that no one ever finds this lagoon. Those fortunate enough to pass by this isolated green hell will never learn its secrets. At the island's core, its overgrown jungle conceals something that aches with a ravenous hunger. A watchful predator, it waits for the next prey to enter its trap. I'm not fully sure what it is. I've only seen glimpses. But I've witnessed its savage effects on its victims. And I've felt its presence taunting me in my nightmares. Should you find this log, do not, under any circumstances, go into the jungle. Leave the island at once.

Skipper Jim Walker opened the hatch and climbed out of the marooned boat. The relentless wind rocked the palm trees, causing their fronds to hiss. In the drizzling rain, he hiked through a thicket of mangroves to the lagoon's beach. He paused before a narrow path that meandered into a jungle so dense, plants and trees fought for space. The dark clouds shrouded the forest in gloom. His heartbeat quickened. In Skipper Jim's frantic mind, every vine-choked tree and bush concealed a predator.

"You want me!" he yelled. "Come get me!" Gripping a fishing knife in his trembling hand, he entered the green hell. He only made it twenty yards before his daughter's voice stopped him. "Hold me, Daddy." Through a mesh of vines and leafy branches, he made out her small camouflaged form stretching out her arms for a hug.

"It's not her," he reminded himself. "Not anymore." *It only speaks with her voice.*

Skipper Jim couldn't stand what the island had done to his baby girl's body. She needed to be properly buried. Tears in his eyes, he approached Ellie with his knife. She didn't try to run, just stood there waiting for Daddy. She began to giggle. And then he suddenly knew this was a trap, his daughter the lure. To his left, branches cracked from a larger body pushing through the jungle, and the thing he feared most sprung from the shadows.

PART ONE

Strangers in Paradise

1

As the fifty-foot yacht sliced through the waterways that ran between the endless maze of Philippine islands, Amy Derwin felt her stomach knot with tension. She gripped the back rail with white knuckles. *Why am I feeling so nervous? I'm on a fancy boat with my best friend and two good-looking men in tropical paradise. I should be having the time of my life.*

But the farther they got from Manila and the safe haven of the resort, the more Amy's breath rose high in her chest; she felt a panicky bird of fear in her throat, trying to get out. Or maybe it was a scream she was desperately holding in.

Jasmine, why do I always let you talk me into things?

She and the guys seemed oblivious as they drank and laughed and carried on like there was nothing to worry about. But Amy felt it, deep in her gut where the knots tightened. Something was very wrong.

It had been too long since they'd seen another boat or an island that showed signs of human habitation. All around them, hills of rock, covered in lush, green vegetation and tropical flowers, rose from the clear blue water. Despite the majestic views, all Amy could think about was what if they got lost out here? Or the boat broke down? She and Jasmine barely knew these men who were taking them to God knew where.

Who goes on a cruise with strange men in a foreign country?
Apparently idiots like us.

2

Two days earlier

As their plane was about to land in Manila, Amy Derwin squeezed her best friend's hand with excitement and still couldn't believe she and Jasmine were actually back together again, after all that had happened.

Amy loved Jasmine Cooper like a sister. More than that, like an extension of herself. They were soul sisters, an invisible cord linking them together for life. When something happened to Jasmine, Amy felt it, and vice versa, like twins feel each other; and they were almost twins, their parents had joked, given that the girls were born minutes apart, only from different mothers. Amy had come into this world quiet and struggling to breathe, the umbilical cord strangling her throat, and nearly died. The doctor attempted to revive her. A minute later, Jasmine practically leaped onto the life stage and screamed so loud her voice carried down the hall of the maternity ward. Amy knew intuitively that Jasmine's triumphant howl for life had saved her. *Jasmine's the reason I'm alive. She's the reason I go on living.*

Amy felt eternal gratitude that their mothers had become friends and raised the girls together from infants to age eleven, until that summer when *the bad thing* happened. The unspeakable thing that forever altered two innocent girls and ripped their families apart. Only the traumatic event didn't stop Amy and Jasmine from staying best friends throughout grade school and college. During their wild and reckless twenties, when they were driven by a need to conquer life and challenge death, Amy and Jasmine had rock-climbed in Sedona, backpacked across Thailand and Bali, explored caves in New Zealand, driven a jeep across Australia's outback with Jasmine standing up and howling, and both of them came within an inch of getting eaten by great white sharks while scuba diving off the Great Barrier Reef. Their daredevil youth kept their friendship tight, feeling invincible. It seemed nothing could stop the force of their sisterhood.

Amy and Jasmine had both shared the same dream to eventually marry and live side by side in their hometown, Ojai, California. Had Amy gone through with her wedding with Michael, Jasmine would have been her maid of honor. Then the girls found the only thing that could ever separate them—Carter Corelli. When Jasmine married Carter, Amy was standing right beside her, despite hating the groom, despite warning Jasmine over and over that this man was wrong for her.

Then came the dark years of their early thirties, when Amy was a hermit living in her condo in Ojai and Jasmine trapped in Carter's emotional prison in an all-glass mansion in Los Angeles. Her asshole husband had screwed with Jasmine's head and convinced her that Amy was a cancer to their marriage. Jasmine then shut Amy out of her life. The dark years, the lonely years, Amy had suffered through long, endless days of silence, wondering about her friend, telepathically feeling her hurt and misery. At the time, Amy feared she'd never be happy again.

But as storms pass, dark years end, and the sun shines again, brightening the world around you with magnificent colors. And you wake up smiling, looking forward to the day, and find it easy to laugh again, to imagine a promising future and so many activities you want to fill it with. For Amy, that day came when Jasmine called her out of the blue. She had finally broken free from Carter's prison and filed for divorce. Crying humble tears, she apologized for letting him come between them and begged for Amy's forgiveness. "Of course, of course," Amy had responded, holding no grudge, just thrilled to hear Jasmine's voice. She asked Amy to travel with her to the Philippines on a much-needed girls' trip. "I want to visit my homeland. Get away from everything. Heal my heart, feel wild and free again, be soul sisters who take life by the balls like we used to. The whole trip is my treat. Will you go with me, Amy? Please! Please!"

Amy had said, "Oh, hell yes!" and dropped everything. *Goodbye dull life, Jasmine is back!*

They had talked non-stop on the flight to Manila, Jasmine sharing all the abuse Carter had put her through, and Amy nodding supportively, holding her friend's hand.

"Carter is a total narcissistic asshole," Amy said. "I'm just beyond happy that you got out, Jazz. I missed you so much."

"I missed you too, Amers."

They both teared up and then Jasmine cracked a joke about Carter's small prick, and the two laughed and cried at the same time.

In Manila, they checked into the Diamond Hotel, where they planned to spend their perfect vacation: relaxing by the pool, spa days, yoga on the beach, shopping at the markets, and riding one of those colorful jeepney buses to tour the city and local villages. Jasmine was half Filipino and had relatives who lived in a small village an hour away from Manila. Amy was very much looking forward to meeting the whole family and immersing herself in their culture.

Yet, two men came along to throw a wrinkle in their plan.

The girls were soaking up the sun by the pool and going over their week's plans when the waiter surprised them with a tray of neon blue rum drinks with fruit garnishes, compliments from two gentlemen at a nearby table. When Amy and Jasmine looked across the pool, the two attractive men raised their own blue drinks. Amy became overwhelmed with nervousness, as if she were back in junior high, which was stupid since she was thirty-four and had dealt with her fair share of men.

Amy's biggest concern was Jasmine, who was vulnerable right now. Men and alcohol often led to broken plans and next-morning regrets. Amy was about to decline the free drinks, but Jasmine quickly took them from the waiter and handed one to Amy.

Jasmine gave the men a little wave. "Mmm, they are cute. Things are about to get interesting."

She started to get up, and Amy grabbed her arm. "Maybe we shouldn't. Those guys are just looking to hook up."

"Maybe that's *exactly* what we both need."

Before Amy could protest, Jasmine walked in her alluring, feminine way around the pool, the men's eyes tracking her every step. She walked right up to their table and began talking with them. A moment later, she waved Amy to come join them.

Amy sighed. *Here we go again.* She put on her wing girl face and joined the other three at the table, who were already chatting and laughing like old friends.

The men introduced themselves as Ted and Dominic, "Dom" for short.

"Small world," Jasmine said. "They're both from L.A. also."

"Yeah, Laurel Canyon," Ted said, giving Amy a lingering look.

"So what brings you two beautiful ladies to the Philippines?" Dom asked.

"We're celebrating my divorce," Jasmine said. "I'm finally a free woman." She left out that she was only legally separated and wouldn't be officially divorced for at least six months.

Amy gave her friend a look, and Jasmine's eyes signaled to go along with it.

Ted said, "I'm divorced myself and so is Dom, so we know what hell marriage can be."

Dom raised his glass. "A toast to your freedom."

They clinked glasses.

"You ever been married?" Ted asked Amy.

The question brought up painful memories. She shook her head. "I came close once."

"Well, you're not missing out on anything," Dom said, "except a lot of heartache and devastation."

"Here, here," Jasmine said and clinked her glass to his again.

The four of them ordered lunch and drank for a couple of hours by the pool. Jasmine, who did most of the talking, shared about growing up with Amy and their childhood dream of starting a custom jewelry business. Amy enjoyed making jewelry out of gold, silver, and gemstones. When they were in their twenties, the girls sold their creations at flea markets and art festivals. Amy was the designer, while Jasmine, who had the gift of gab, could sell jewelry to anyone.

"Amy's so creative," Jasmine said enviously. "Some of the pieces she designs blow my mind. She made this." She held up a gold chain necklace with a golden dragon wrapped around a jade stone that matched her green eyes.

Hearing Jasmine talking excitedly about opening up their shop in Ojai got Amy feeling good about their future. *Maybe we'll actually make it successful this time.*

Ted and Dom turned out to be more interesting than Amy's first impression. They didn't come across as the usual horny douchebags who hit on her and Jasmine to get one thing out of them. Both men were very relaxed and casual, confident. They were movie producers scouting locations in the Philippines to shoot a film on a remote tropical island. Ted's father was a famous Hollywood movie director, and Ted helped run the production company. Dom was an assistant producer and screenwriter and did some acting.

"I mostly do comedy," he said, doing a goofy Jim Carrey impression and making Jasmine snort with laughter. She kept touching Dom's arm. He was boyishly cute with lean, tanned muscles, spiky dark hair, brown eyes, and a playful personality. He flirted back, making Jasmine giggle like Amy hadn't heard in a long time. The laughter was infectious, or maybe it was the number of rum drinks they were putting away, but Amy found herself cracking up at Dom's crazy stories about working in Hollywood.

Ted was more reserved and carried himself with a quiet confidence. His deep-set, intelligent eyes were difficult to read. More than once, his penetrating gaze locked onto Amy. She felt self-conscious, as if he could see into her and observe all her flaws.

He knows your big secret. He can see where you're damaged. As she thought this, he smiled at her, the kind of smile that can make a woman feel both sexy and suddenly bashful. That smile sent ripples up her chest. She felt curiously attracted to Ted, yet wary. He was a few years older, forty-two, and carried himself like a man who had traveled the globe and been with many women. He alluded to the fact that he had been married more than once and was happily divorced. Afraid of sending the wrong signals, Amy was careful not to flirt too much and only made brief eye contact when talking to him.

After lunch by the pool, the guys took Amy and Jasmine shopping in the hotel's boutique. Ted, who paid for everything with a platinum card, insisted on buying the women expensive bikinis, hats, sunglasses, tropical Roberto Cavalli dresses, and high-heeled shoes. Amy didn't feel right about accepting all the gifts, but Jasmine, who was used to being pampered by rich men, encouraged Amy to enjoy being treated like a princess.

That night, after the girls donned their new dresses and shoes, the guys treated them to a high-priced dinner and drinks at the hotel's karaoke bar. Jasmine and Dom kept everyone entertained, singing duets that got more slurred as the night went on. Then they got down and dirty on the dance floor, Jasmine grinding her hips against Dom, while Amy and Ted sat at the table and talked, Ted mostly. Amy was too distracted as she watched her friend. Occasionally, Ted sat a little too close and Amy inched away. A panicky feeling began to fill her chest. Everything was happening too fast, their vacation spinning out of control. She had wanted a low-key day reading a book and spending quality time with Jasmine. Amy only tagged along as wing girl to make sure her friend didn't get herself into trouble.

Now, Jasmine and Dom were kissing hard on the dance floor, sloppy and embarrassing, the way drunks make out.

Amy abandoned Ted and walked onto the dance floor. She tugged on Jasmine's arm, interrupting her and Dom's kissing. "Come on, girl, let's go."

Jasmine gave her an angry, drunken glare. "What?"

"It's time we went back to our room."

"Go ahead. I'm having fun."

Amy bristled at her friend's defiance. "You've had too much to drink. I think it's best we call it a night."

"No, I don't want to."

The girls stared hard at one another in a momentary standoff. Amy had hoped Jasmine had grown out of this. She clung on to Dom. "I'm going to sleep in Dom's room." She caressed his chest. "Is that all right, Dommy?"

He grinned like a guy who'd just won the lottery. "All right with me." Swaying and glassy eyed, he said to Amy in a John Wayne voice, "Don't worry, missy. I'll look after the little lady."

"I'm sure you will, Dom, but my friend and I have a big day planned tomorrow. We need to get to sleep. Come along, sister." Amy grabbed her hand, but Jasmine jerked it away.

"Go to bed, if you want, but I'm staying. Come on, Dommy, let's move this party to your room," Jasmine pulled him off the dance floor, and the two stumbled out of the bar like drunken sailors.

Lights flashing, disco ball swirling, couples dancing to a Filipino man singing bad karaoke, Amy stood on the dance floor, feeling abandoned, pissed off, and worried. *I should go after her. Drag her ass back to our room and lock her in with me.* Amy was terrified how Jasmine would respond. Their friendship had been so fragile through the dark years that Amy was afraid to test it. She could hear the corrupted Jasmine saying, "Carter's right, you're always trying to control me. You're always suffocating me. I think we need some space apart. Don't call me."

If Jasmine said that again and suddenly ended their friendship, Amy didn't know what she would do. She couldn't go through the dark years again.

Jasmine's not a girl anymore, Amy reasoned. *She's a grown woman on the rebound from a bad marriage. Maybe she needs this fling. Get all the shit out of her system that Carter put her through. You want your best friend back, then you have to accept her wild side.* And Amy knew from past experience that when Wild Jasmine appeared, there was nothing she could do to stop her friend.

As a woman began singing a slow love song, Ted tapped Amy on the shoulder. "Care to dance?"

Amy looked at him, feeling bad that she had left him at the table in the middle of him telling a story. "Sorry, I'm not feeling up to it."

"How about I order us a bottle of champagne and we take a walk along the beach."

Amy politely turned him down. She thanked him for dinner, said goodnight, then went to bed, alone.

3

At 4:00 a.m., Jasmine turned on a lamp and bounced onto Amy's bed, waking her up. "Guess what, sister? Dom and Ted invited us to tour the islands on their yacht!"

"When?"

"We leave in an hour, so get dressed."

Amy crossed her arms. "I thought you and I were going to spend the day at the spa."

"Yacht beats spa any day. Besides, we've got all week to hang at the hotel. I'd rather go with them to scout islands for their movie. Let's go have an adventure!"

"You already told them yes, didn't you?" Amy said, feeling a flash of heat radiating beneath her skin.

"I figured you'd want to go with us. So I kinda told the guys we'd meet them in the lobby. Say you'll go, please, please, please... I really like Dom, and I could tell that Ted is into you."

"I don't know, Jazz, we barely know them."

"I got to know Dom really well last night." Jasmine beamed. "He definitely gave me my groove back. The guy's got a freaking anaconda between his legs, and he knows how to use it."

Amy pushed her arm. "Shut up, slut."

"It's the longest I've ever seen. And it's *un*-circumcised. You should see it."

"I'll pass. And thanks for putting that image in my head."

"What do you think of Ted?"

Amy shrugged. "He seems nice enough, but he did come on a little strong."

"So, did you guys…?" Jasmine bounced her eyebrows.

"God no! As you can see, I slept alone."

"You can't sleep with pillow man forever."

Amy laughed, looking at the long pillow she'd been snuggling. "It's worked so far."

"You should give Ted a chance. You need to get laid in the worst way."

"Hah, says the slut. You're just projecting your own carnal needs."

"Seriously, Amers, it's been over four years, since Michael, you know…"

"I know, but I still miss him." Amy's mind couldn't shake the painful memories of her fiancé's wrecked car, watching his coffin being lowered into the ground. Since she'd lost the only man she'd ever loved, Amy hadn't even thought of dating. The idea of being intimate with any man other than Michael felt wrong. Her pillow man was the only substitute for sleeping in his arms.

"If you're ever going to move on, Amy, this vacation is the perfect place to do it."

"I can't jump into bed with a strange guy like you do. I have to get to know him first. Date him a few months. Check his criminal record."

Jasmine gripped Amy's hands and shook her arms. "Come on, sister. Sow some wild oats. You deserve to live it up, for once. Get to know Ted today on the yacht. By tonight, he might make you feel as happy as Dom makes me feel."

4

While the yacht carved a watery path through the maze of islands and Amy brooded on the back deck, Jasmine joined her, throwing her arm around her shoulder. "Hey, you okay?"

"Sure, fine," Amy lied.

"Something's bothering you."

Amy made sure Ted and Dom were out of earshot, then whispered, "What if we're wrong about these guys? What if they turn out to be serial killers? Out here, no one would ever find our bodies."

"Stop thinking such morbid thoughts," Jasmine whispered. "You're scaring yourself. Dom and Ted are harmless. They have been nothing but gentlemen."

"Guys can be deceiving," Amy said, one eyebrow arched.

"Not all men are like Boyd and Carter." Jasmine pulled a beer can out of a cooler and offered it to Amy. "Try to relax and have some fun with us."

Jasmine bumped her hip against Amy's and got her to smile. Then Jasmine walked along the starboard to the bow of the boat and lay on her beach towel beside Dom.

Amy sighed. Underneath her fear was a disappointment in herself that she was spoiling their vacation. *You promised yourself that you'd have a good time with her. Like it or not, you're on this cruise with Jasmine, her date, and his friend.*

Relax and have fun for Jasmine. That was Amy's mantra for this trip, even if it meant pushing out of her comfort zone and being on a double date.

Amy went back inside the upper deck cabin. To her right was a galley that looked fancier than her kitchen at home, with sleek wood panels, black countertops, and built-in appliances. To her left, a long white leather couch lined the wall and curved around the dining table on three sides. The side windows offered plenty of natural light.

Just past the galley, at the helm, Ted manned the wheel, steering the fifty-foot yacht along the channel between two cliffs. He looked comfortable behind the wheel, as if he'd grown up around boats. Dressed in an unbuttoned Tommy Bahama shirt, a navy tank top underneath, khaki shorts, flip-flops, and a white skipper's hat, Ted reminded Amy of a boatman who might live in Key West and listen to Jimmy Buffet all day. Ted was fit for a man in his early forties. His toned muscles were bronzed by the sun. His sculpted legs looked as if he cycled or played tennis. His short blond hair had flecks of gray at the temples, giving him a distinguished look.

Amy felt guilty for finding him attractive, as if Michael were watching from above, disapproving. Ted, all chiseled and sophisticated, was so unlike her fiancé. Michael had been tall and a little overweight, like a big, huggable bear. He was a blue-collar country boy from Texas, outdoorsy, unrefined, with a great sense of humor, and so full of life, always whisking Amy off to go country-western dancing, camping, fishing, or tour breweries. In his garage, he had brewed his own brand of the most bitter beer, which Amy, who was a wine drinker, eventually acquired a taste for. And his husky laugh and the way he had smiled at her always made her feel all giddy inside. Michael had been the first person besides Jasmine that Amy had let into her heart. The first and only man she had felt safe enough to be intimate with.

Amy caught herself getting lost in the memories, realizing once again that she was comparing a guy to Michael.

When Ted turned and saw her approaching, his blues eyes lit up. "There you are. I was wondering where you went."

"Just outside to get some air."

"Are you seasick? There's some Bonine in the first-aid kit."

"I'm fine. I think it was more the balmy heat getting to me. I feel better, just a little thirsty." She grabbed a bottled water from the fridge and took a drink.

Ted faced the front window again, concentrating on turning the boat around an atoll. An awkward silence fell between them. *Talk to him,* Amy urged herself. It had been so long since she'd been on a date, she didn't quite know what to say. She was curious about Ted, but didn't want him to get the wrong idea and think she was *that* interested. In the past, whenever Jasmine had one-night stands with men, their friends always assumed Amy would have sex with them. It was always a juggle, wanting to be sexy and seen for her beauty as well as her mind, but not wanting to have to fend off aggressive men.

Amy stood next to the dining table, looking out the windows, trying to think of something to get Ted talking. "So…where did you learn how to drive a boat?"

"We always had yachts when I was growing up in Santa Barbara. My parents liked to entertain movie people."

"You must have met a lot of celebrities."

He nodded like it was no big deal. "Hollywood people may seem glamorous on the big screen, but most of them are shallow and screwed up. I watched them do a lot of drugs. My father liked to challenge people to coke-snorting races. He and his friends would smoke cigars, drink Scotch, and my father's raucous laugh would rise above the party." Ted shook his head, as if remembering. "I got along better with the crew. We had an Irish skipper named Tully who took me under his wing. He taught me how to operate a yacht from bow to stern, tie boating knots, and fish. Whenever we cruised the French Riviera or the Greek isles, I probably spent more time with Tully than I did my own father."

She sensed some bitterness in his voice. "But you work with your dad now, right? You must see him all the time."

"Hardly ever, actually. He's always traveling and directing movies. I mostly run the production company from L.A., work with Dom on scripts, and do the initial scouting for my father's next feature. I occasionally get a text from him to contact an actor or hire a crew, schmooze at some party, but that's about the extent of our relationship."

Amy felt like she had steered Ted into a dark, uncomfortable place, so she changed tack. "What about your mother? What's she like?"

Ted's faced hardened even more, and he took a few seconds to respond. "Mother was a soap opera star in the nineties and early two thousands. You may have heard of her, Jacqueline Northcott."

"From *As the World Turns*," Amy said. "Oh, yes, I remember her. She was one of my favorite characters until they killed her off. I always wondered what happened to her."

"She retired after her nervous breakdown. Now, she mostly throws charity benefits and socials, which are excuses to drink martinis with her alcoholic friends."

"Oh, I didn't know."

The hardness of his face softened. He smiled self-consciously. "Sorry, didn't mean to be such a downer. Truth is, it was difficult growing up with Hollywood parents. I missed out on that close family relationship I see other people having."

Amy felt compassion for Ted, because she had been ignored by her own parents, who were stoned half the time and rarely present. Seeing that he could be vulnerable, she relaxed a little.

He patted the black leather seat next to him. "Join me. I'll show you how to captain this bad boy."

Amy sat beside Ted. He gave her a brief explanation of the gauges, digital screens of the elaborate control panel, and the VHF marine radio for communicating with other vessels. Then he let her take the wheel. The power of the boat vibrated in her hands. A wraparound windshield offered a view of the bow nosing through the narrow channel ahead.

Sunbathing on the bow next to Dom, Jasmine waved when she saw that Amy was driving. "You go, girl!"

Amy smiled and gave a thumbs up.

Jasmine watched her friend distractedly. *I hope she's enjoying herself. She needs this trip as much as I do. Maybe more so.*

It wasn't healthy, clinging to Michael's ghost. Jasmine was really hoping Ted was just the man to help Amy finally move on. *Are you sure he's right for her?* He was so different than Michael, who had been completely outgoing, the life of the party, a kind man who wore his heart on his sleeve. You always knew where you stood with Michael. He and Jasmine had sometimes butted heads, but whether he was being hot-headed or treating Jasmine like family, she had appreciated his authenticity.

Ted seemed a bit too cool in his mannerisms, like he watched the world from inside his protective shell, but he also had been a gentleman and extremely generous. He knew how to pamper women and make them feel special, which scored him bonus points. Ted and Dom might have been too L.A. for a couple of small-town girls, but who cared? Neither of these men were the kind you got serious with, but perfect for fun flings while on vacation and getting over tragic relationships. The wounds from fighting with Carter were still fresh.

Some moments, in between the drinking and the laughter, the pain and sadness would seep through. Carter's shouting voice would echo inside Jasmine's head, calling her a stupid bitch, gold-digger, whore, every name he could think of to hurt her.

"You seem a million miles away," Dom said, nudging her.

"Sorry. I've had a lot on my mind." She shook her head and looked out at a passing island. "Man, divorce sucks."

"I hear ya. After mine, I was constantly replaying my marriage in my head, wondering what went wrong."

"You ever figure it out?"

"Some people just don't mix. What was he like, your ex?"

"Oh, don't get me started. Talking about him will spoil the party."

"Seriously, I'll listen if want to share. If not, no worries."

She studied Dom a moment and saw that there was sincere interest in his beautiful brown eyes. "In hindsight, I made the mistake of marrying a narcissistic sociopath. A cruel, woman-hating prick. He acted like Mr. Perfect while we were dating. Then, after we got married, the mask came off to reveal the monster he truly was. He constantly told me I was a shitty wife. Truth was, I had gone overboard to please Carter, was faithful to him, cooked for him, kept the house immaculate, made myself sexually available, and he still played mind games and fucked around."

"The bastard," Dom said.

"Oh, it gets worse. For years I had suspected he was seeing other women, but he always denied it. A few weeks ago, I discovered his secret folder on his computer. It contained photos of dozens of women, all organized in folders titled *Blondes, Brunettes, Redheads*. Several of the photos were selfies of Carter naked in bed or a hot tub with his arm around his mistress of the moment. I found my own nude photos, taken on our honeymoon, collected in a folder titled *Hot Asians*, along with several nameless women from his business trips to Thailand and Hong Kong."

Jasmine shared how her heart had been crushed. Her identity as Mrs. Carter Corelli blown to a million pieces. The more she dug deeper into her husband's secret life, the more she realized everything he ever told her was a lie. She found flirtatious emails discussing meet-ups for sex and a dozen profiles on online dating accounts, from sites that matched sugar daddies with sugar babies to kink communities that involved bondage and S&M. He was a member of the Bacchus Gold Club, a secret wealthy men's club that arranged parties with high-end prostitutes.

Enraged, Jasmine had printed the emails and profiles, copied all the photos to a thumb drive, and hired a divorce attorney. After two weeks, the divorce had already gotten ugly. Carter was using every manipulative tactic in his arsenal to wear her down, from tearing apart her character to begging her to forgive him and come home, promising that he'd change. Jasmine's self-esteem had been so low, that she almost went back to him. But with Amy's support and a pit-bull attorney, Jasmine was holding strong. Carter no longer had the power to hurt her.

Dom squeezed her hand. "Good for you for getting out. I'm sorry you went through all that."

She intertwined her fingers with his. "I know after it's all over and the divorce is final, I'll be a stronger person. Anyway, my nightmare marriage is in the rearview mirror. From now on, I'm going to live life as I please."

Dom smiled. "Does that include more of what we did last night?"

Jasmine nodded and kissed his lips. "A lot more."

When the channel split off into a cluster of jutting rocks, Ted took the wheel again. Through the side windows, Amy watched countless islands drift by, some covered with jungles, others small budding atolls of coral rock speckled with greenery and resting birds.

"You know how many islands are in the Philippines?" Ted asked her. "Over seven thousand, five hundred by the latest count. And only two thousand are inhabited." He smiled. "The other fifty-five hundred islands are *ours* to explore." His tone turned unexpectedly intimate, as if he was already feeling familiar with her.

"All the islands look the same," Amy said. "How do you not get lost out here?"

Ted tapped the side of his head. "I have a sixth sense for navigation."

The boat entered a stretch of open water, and he increased the speed. The bow bounced on the waves. Dom and Jasmine cheered as they held onto their hats and beers.

"Where are we going exactly?" Amy asked Ted.

"The screenplay calls for a remote island that is uninhabited with lush jungles."

"We've passed several like that so far." Amy wished he'd pick a place to stop. They'd already been cruising for six hours, getting farther and farther away from Manila.

Ted pointed to the GPS screen. "Map shows another cluster of islands up ahead. These are what interest me. I talked to some local fishermen. They spoke of a group of islands they steer clear of. *Masasamang isla*, they call them. Evil islands."

"*That's* where you want to go?" Amy asked.

"We're producing a horror film, so what better place than an island that spooks the locals? Dom and I have been working some of the Filipino legends into the script. The rural villagers are extremely superstitious and take their folklore literally. In a barangay outside of Manila, I witnessed the village people putting out bowls of food for *duwende*, little goblins they claim feed off humans. There are areas of jungle the villagers avoid, because they are terrified of encountering a blood-sucking *aswang,* a cross-between a vampire and a witch, or a giant *kapre,* a sort of ogre. According to folklore, many of these islands inhabit mythical monsters."

Amy let out a nervous laugh. "And you believe these superstitions?"

"No, but there have been reports of people going missing in this archipelago. That's why you don't see a lot of fishermen here. Only foreign boaters like ourselves are daring enough to venture into this cluster."

Amy didn't believe in folklore monsters, but it made her nervous going to a place where there had been disappearances. "Maybe we should heed the fishermen's warnings."

"Don't worry, you're safe with me." Ted stroked her back. His touch made every muscle in her body stiffen.

At the next labyrinth of islands and water passages, Ted slowed the boat to a gentle cruise speed. He remained quiet, his eyes working as he searched the passing atolls.

Amy watched out a side window. The lush green rocks, rising from coral shelves, were covered in jungle plants. A breeze carried the scent of salt water and flowers. Some of the islands had empty beaches and dense jungles. Monkeys hooted and shook the tree branches. Fairy-bluebirds flew from one isle to the next. Several of the bigger islands were bordered with thick mangroves that prevented any access to the land.

Ted said, "Whoa, here we go." He steered the yacht toward a narrow channel that cut through a thick wall of mangroves. The passage was barely wide enough for the boat to squeeze through. Amy began to feel claustrophobic, like the island was swallowing them down its snake-long throat.

Dom and Jasmine stood on the bow.

"How deep does the water look?" Ted asked.

"Deep enough!" Dom yelled. "Keep going. This place looks perfect!"

After a couple hundred yards of weaving through mangrove forest, the passage opened up to a hidden lagoon. The water was so clear, Amy could see seaweed swaying at the sandy bottom.

Ted backed the boat up to sixty yards from the island's shore and stuck his head out a window. "Anchors aweigh!"

Dom released the anchor. Ted shut off the engine, and the four of them gathered on the back deck, which faced the most breathtaking white sand beach, insulated by thick jungle, tall palm trees, and looming cliffs.

Ted waved a hand toward the lagoon. "Welcome to our own private paradise."

5

While Amy and Jasmine were below deck in the master cabin, changing into their new bathing suits, one of the men snuck into the hallway bathroom.

Finally, the moment I've been waiting for.

He pulled out an iPad and tapped an app, accessing the hidden camera in the next room. The two women appeared on the small screen, half-naked. The voyeur felt a rush of excitement. Amy stood a few inches taller than Jasmine and had a lean, toned yoga body with a narrow waist. Amy was already topless, wearing only her blue bikini bottoms, but had her back to the camera.

The man licked his lips. *Turn around. Let me see you.*

To his delight, Jasmine peeled off her own clothes until she was fully naked.

Oh, yes… He instantly turned bolt-hard. He stroked himself.

The Asian chick was petite and slender and tan all over. Her long black hair hung past her shoulders. He loved her plump tits with those small brown nipples. He already had a sex video of her from last night. The way Jasmine fucked drove him wild. She was comfortable with her nakedness as she talked to her friend. The man's lust amped up as he admired the trimmed, dark jungle of pubic hair between Jasmine's legs as she slid her bikini bottoms up her thighs and over her hips. He had been with his fair share of Asians on trips to Thailand, Vietnam, and the Philippines. Women like Jasmine were fun for a few bangs, but his preference was full-blooded American women, especially blondes like Amy. He had wanted her from the second he spotted her sitting across the pool. Fuck, he wanted her *right now.*

The cocktease still hadn't turned around, as if Amy somehow sensed the camera hidden near the bedroom mirror was recording her for his collection. The man's eyes followed her braided ponytail down her bare back. The way Amy's bikini bottoms hugged her tight little ass made it difficult to look at anything else. He imagined bending her over, taking her from behind, while her friend watched. He stroked himself, faster and harder. He had to see Amy's breasts. A flash of anger fused with his desire. Heat shot from his forehead down to his cock and balls, which had swollen to near bursting.

Turn around, damn it! Let me see those tits!

Her back still turned, Amy put on her bikini top, and Jasmine tied the strings for her. Amy finally turned around, but all the parts he wanted to see were covered. The hugging fabric revealed that Amy's perky breasts had a firm shape to them. The voyeur couldn't wait to squeeze them and suck them, and do so much more to Amy. Jasmine too. Yes, take turns with them.

What about his friend? Well, he could join the party too. It wouldn't be the first time they'd shared.

Would the women play along?

Of course they would. All women were nymphos in disguise. When on vacation, they let out their wild and horny sides. Jasmine sure let out hers last night. Amy was more closed off, but she just needed the right man to get her hot. A few drinks and a little coke and X also helped with letting go of inhibitions. Soon he would be seeing Amy fully naked and doing more than just looking. This tropical island was the perfect setting to live out his wildest fantasies. There was not a soul around for miles out here.

Amy and Jasmine peered into the bedroom mirror, unknowingly facing the camera. They seemed to stare right at him as they primped their hair and rolled lip balm across their sexy mouths.

He stroked so hard he almost exploded. He stopped himself, squeezing off the surge until his testicles hurt. *Save it for them.*

6

In the saloon, Amy and Jasmine chatted and listened to music as they packed sandwiches, chips, and snack bars into a beach bag. Dom entered the galley and put his arms around their shoulders. "I think I'm in Heaven. How about we ditch Ted and you girls run off into the jungle with me. We'll unleash our primal natures."

"I'm game." Jasmine bumped Amy's hip. "How about it, girlfriend? Ready to play Sheena of the jungle?"

"More like Betty on the beach. You two can run through palm fronds all you want. I'm going to lay out and enjoy the book I brought."

"Ah, you're no fun," Dom said.

"Be happy, you're with the adventurous one," Amy said. "Besides, I'd feel bad if we abandoned Ted."

"My ears are burning." Ted came in from the back deck. "What are you three talking about?"

"Just getting our lunch ready," Amy said. "Want a beer?"

"Would love one."

She tossed him a cold can. Since she was spending the next few hours on an island with Ted and Dom and her best friend, Amy decided to relax and enjoy herself.

Ted's fingers grazed the small of her back as he stepped up behind her. "Ready to have some fun?"

"Getting there." Amy chugged the rest of her beer. It would take a lot of these to resurrect her wild side.

The four adventurers gathered on the swim platform.

Ted jumped into the water. "Ah, feels great. Hop in, guys."

Dom opened a back storage compartment that revealed a small inflatable motorboat. "Aren't we going to take the dinghy?"

"Nah," Ted said. "It's not that far. We can swim to the beach."

"Sure, I'm game." Amy dove into the crystal clear water. A forest of kelp swayed along the sandy bottom. A natural born water baby and lifelong swimmer, Amy felt at home as a mermaid underwater. She resurfaced beside Jasmine, who was treading water.

Only Dom remained on the boat, apprehensive.

"You're not afraid of the water, are you, Dommy?" Ted challenged.

"No, and don't call me that, or I'll be calling you *Teddy*."

"Fine, jump in already."

"What about getting our food and drinks to shore?"

"That's what the floating cooler is for, jackass." Ted shook his head, and said to the girls, "Can't take him anywhere."

Dom gave his friend the finger.

Amy and Ted raced each other toward the beach. Ted zipped ahead of her, swimming freestyle. He had nice form.

Farther back, Dom took his sweet time as he swam and pushed the floating cooler full of beers, water, and sodas. On top, sat their beach bag packed with towels and food.

Jasmine swam slowest, dogpaddling and kicking her legs out like a frog. She had on her new floppy sunhat and big Gucci sunglasses.

Amy preferred a sportier look with her Oakleys and sun visor. Her braided ponytail was already soaked from doing backstrokes. After being on the hot boat, the cool water felt invigorating. Amy spun around and switched to breaststrokes. Soon her feet found the sandy bottom that sloped toward the beach. The sun warmed her damp chest and back as she waded waist deep. The underwater seaweed tickled her legs.

Ted sat in the shallow water, waiting for the others to catch up. "You can really swim," he told Amy as she approached. "Do you compete?"

"Thanks, I did back in high school. Also worked summers as a lifeguard." She was still breathing heavy from the exertion. "I was thinking I had you beat. How did you learn to swim so fast?"

"Twice a year I race triathlons," Ted said. "I usually win my age bracket."

"Impressive," Amy said, unimpressed with his bragging.

She stopped just short of the shore to take in the view. On either side, palm trees, mangroves, and white sand beaches curved around them to form a mostly enclosed lagoon. Straight ahead, beyond the narrow beach, stretched a shadowy jungle overgrown with vegetation.

"Oh, I love it here." Jasmine waded up beside Dom and grabbed her phone from her beach bag, which sat atop the floating cooler. She took photos with her phone. "Absolutely breathtaking."

Amy didn't share her friend's enthusiasm. The island seemed beautiful on the surface, but something felt off. She got the skin-prickling sensation that something in the dense forest was watching them as they walked ashore.

"Did you guys see that?" Amy pointed to the thicket of trees off to their left. "Something moved the branches."

"Probably a bird," Dom said.

"Or monkeys," Jasmine added. "I hope we see some."

The shape that retreated into the jungle seemed larger than a monkey. "You guys sure there aren't *people* living here?" Amy asked.

Ted snorted. "I doubt any of the islands in this area are inhabited. I took us *way* off the beaten path."

"Of course, there's always the chance a tribe of headhunters could be living here." A mischievous grin spread over Dom's face.

Ted nodded. "We are close enough to Papua New Guinea that headhunters could have made their way up to these parts. Bet they're in the jungle sharpening their machetes."

"Stop, you're creeping me out," Amy said.

Dom nudged her. "If a headhunter pops out of the jungle, I'll protect you."

"With what?" she joked. "Hit him over the head with a cooler?"

"You're looking at a black belt in Tae Kwon Do. No headhunter stands a chance against these lethal hands." Dom mimicked a few karate chops and kicked his leg out of the water.

Jasmine laughed. "I feel safer already."

Amy helped the others drag the floating cooler onto the beach. They laid out towels and set up their picnic. While enjoying the view of the lagoon, they ate sandwiches and chips and drank cold beer.

Amy looked at Jasmine. "This place reminds me of the time we visited that beach in Thailand. Remember the Phi Phi Islands, Jazz? You just *had* to visit Monkey Beach."

Jasmine laughed. "It sounded so fun at the time."

Amy laughed with her, and they both shook their heads.

"What happened?" Ted asked.

"We rented kayaks and paddled to a hidden cove called Monkey Bay," Amy said. "There's a secluded beach there where tourists go to feed wild monkeys."

"We brought bunches of bananas with us," Jasmine said. "I expected the monkeys to be small and sweet. Boy was I ever wrong."

Amy chuckled. "You should have seen Jasmine walking toward them with an armload of bananas. A crowd of about thirty monkeys swarmed her."

"There were some big ones too," Jasmine added. "And they were jumping all over me, grabbing at the bananas, my hair, my bathing suit."

"She started squealing," Amy said. "I could barely see Jasmine beneath the horde. The monkeys snatched all her bananas and stole her bikini top too. Jazz ran screaming down the beach topless with a pack of monkeys clinging to her. There must have been twenty tourists there taking photos of her."

"I would've loved to have seen that," Dom said.

"You can find plenty of videos of it on YouTube," Jasmine said, shaking her head.

Amy nudged her shoulder. "I warned her, monkeys are aggressive, but does she listen to her wise girlfriend?"

Jasmine looked toward the jungle. "I wonder where the monkeys are on this island? You'd think they'd be approaching us, expecting to be fed."

"They probably aren't used to visitors," Ted said. "As soon as they saw our boat, I bet they retreated inland."

After lunch, they split off into pairs to search for wood to build a fire for later that evening. The guys walked down one end of the beach, and the girls down the other.

Jasmine picked up a piece of driftwood. "So how are thing's cooking with you and Ted?"

"We haven't even reached a simmer," Amy said.

"It looked like you two were getting chummy on the boat."

"He was telling me how he got into yachting and that the boat we were on is small compared to his family's 100-foot yacht in Santa Barbara. He keeps trying to impress me."

"Of course, Amers, he likes you. You should give Ted a chance."

"I'll try, but don't get your hopes up. Attraction can't be forced." Amy spotted something in the woods that looked manmade. "What is *that*?" She wandered into a grove of trees. Set back in the shadows was a shack constructed from green logs and palm fronds.

"Cool," Jasmine said. "A tiki hut. Maybe it has a bar that serves tropical drinks."

"It's so hot I could go for a piña colada right about now."

When they got closer and saw the condition of the hut, Jasmine released a sound of disappointment. "No such luck."

The one-room shack sat on stilts two feet off the ground. It had a wide-open front with no door, just two side walls and a back wall made of twined sticks. A thatch roof covered the shelter. Dead palm fronds and leaves littered the gloomy interior. It reeked of mildew. A lime green fungus grew along the front posts. From the ceiling hung several vines strung through old monkey skulls, three and four heads to a vine. The creepy totems twirled in the breeze.

"Gross." Amy got goose bumps. "Think some monkey headhunter still lives here?"

Jasmine poked her head inside the hut. "It doesn't exactly have a lived-in look. There's no furniture, and everything's covered in mold and lichen."

"I can't shake the bad feeling we're trespassing on somebody's private beach." Amy looked past the hut to the thick wall of foliage behind it. "There could be a house set farther in the jungle. A hermit who hates trespassers might come after us with a gun."

"You're being paranoid again."

"I'm being sensible. Out here there aren't any police to protect us. Not to mention we're in a remote part of a foreign country where the locals live by their own laws."

Jasmine's brow knitted. "Let's see what the guys think."

They returned to the beach and called the men over. They came running.

"Well, would you look at that?" Dom said, approaching the hut. "Someone's been here after all."

Ted climbed inside. His feet clumped over rotted boards. "Nice decor." He tapped one of the monkey-skull vines and sent it swinging.

"I think we found Tarzan's man cave," Dom joked.

"Whoever lived here left this behind." In the back corner, Ted picked up a rusty machete. "Shit, it's covered in something sticky." He tossed the long knife back on the floor and wiped his hand on his bathing suit, smudging it with a green stain.

Amy explained her hermit theory, that maybe they were trespassing on someone's privately owned island.

"Maybe Dr. Moreau has a house back there," Dom teased. "The mad scientist is turning people into animals, and we're next."

Jasmine elbowed his ribs.

"I doubt anyone owns this rock," Ted said. "I drove us into an area of unchartered islands. I guess it's possible someone got shipwrecked and has been living here as a hermit."

Dom laughed. "He's probably half-naked, except for a few monkey skins."

"This is no time to joke," Amy said. "The presence of this hut raises a serious safety concern."

"Wonder who it belongs to," Jasmine said.

"Looks like it's been here for decades," Ted said. "I read that back in World War II platoons of Japanese soldiers got left behind on these islands. They built shelters and survived as long as they could. They eventually ran out of food and turned into savages." With a straight face, he added, "They filed their teeth down to points and cannibalized one another."

"There might be one old, fang-toothed cannibal left," Dom said. "He could be in the jungle, stalking us right now with a spear."

"He'd be near a hundred years old," Ted said.

"I heard eating human meat gives people superhuman strength," Dom said, grinning.

"Quit jacking around or I'm going back to the boat," Amy said.

"Yeah," Jasmine said, "this is no place for cannibal jokes."

"Lighten up, ladies," Ted said. "We're just pulling your chains. The hut clearly hasn't been used in ages. There's no sign of a campfire."

"I'm sure our monkey-killing hermit's long gone by now," Dom said.

"How can you guys be so sure?" Amy said. "We've only seen one side of the island."

"You're right, we need to get the lay of the land." Ted stepped around the corner and Dom followed.

"There's a path over here," Ted called and started into the jungle. It was so thick the intertwining treetops cast deep shadows in places the sun struggled to reach. There was no telling how deep the tropical forest went.

"We should just stick to the beach," Amy suggested.

Ignoring her, the men pushed their way between big elephant-ear plants and disappeared.

Jasmine started to follow.

"What are you doing?" Amy asked.

"Exploring with the guys. You don't have to come with us. You're free to go back to the beach and be Queen Stick-in-the-Mud."

Her friend's sarcastic tone cut deep. "Maybe I will." Amy crossed her arms. "I can see my vote counts for nothing with you three." She looked away to hide her face. Her lip always trembled when her feelings got hurt.

Jasmine approached and touched her arm. "I'm sorry, Amers. I just want you to loosen up and have fun with us."

"I'm trying, but this island really makes me uncomfortable."

"What about it is so scary? We're in paradise."

"Something feels off… The jungle's too quiet. There are no bird sounds, no monkeys…and that hut with the skulls and the machete…"

"I admit that's a bit weird, but it does look abandoned." Jasmine looked around. "Even if there was some old hermit on the island, I'd feel safer if we all stuck together. Do you really want to go sit on the beach alone?"

"What I *want* is for you and me to be lounging by the hotel pool and drinking daiquiris like we planned."

"We will, as soon as we get back. Until then, let's have an adventure."

Amy reluctantly followed her friend into the jungle. Under the canopy of trees, balmy air caused perspiration to bead on their backs. The remnant of a path was mostly overgrown with branches. The only sounds were their feet passing over the damp dirt floor and the slap of wet leaves as the four pushed through the jungle. Bushes and tree branches clotted around them, obscuring the view. Areas beyond twenty feet were cast in a deep gray gloom. Again, Amy got a prickling sensation they were being watched. Was someone crouched between two bushes? She focused on that spot, watching for movement. The shape was the stump of a long dead trunk. Aware of her heartbeat, sweat streaming down her back, she followed the others deeper into the trees.

At last the jungle opened up to a second lagoon. This one was completely enclosed by land, like an oasis. The still water was so clear that Amy could see a thick bed of seaweed just below the surface. She didn't see a single fish. Like the jungle, the lagoon seemed devoid of animal life.

"Holy shit, would you look at that?" Dom shouted.

Up the beach, the wreckage of a large wooden ship, covered in ivy, leaned on its side in the sand.

Dom, Ted, and Jasmine rounded the lagoon toward the ship. Amy followed. The faded planked hull, still intact except for a few holes, loomed above them.

Jasmine took a step back and craned her head. "The hull looks like a pirate's ship."

Dom spoke in a pirate's voice, "Arg, maybe this place is like that Michael Caine movie, *The Island*. It could be inhabited by cutthroat buccaneers."

Jasmine rolled her eyes. "Oh, please."

Dom walked to the edge of the trees and shouted, "Are there any pirates on this island?"

"Knock it off, Dom," Jasmine warned.

He gave her a boyish grin.

"It's a Filipino fishing boat," Ted said, touching the prow. "Most of the paint and fiberglass has chipped away, exposing the wood hull beneath. To be beached in this enclosed lagoon, it must have been here at least a decade."

"And no one's discovered it before us?" Amy said. "I find that hard to believe."

"An island this remote can go years without anyone exploring it," Ted said. "The jungle's mostly overtaken it, so the wreckage would be hard to spot from a plane."

Ted was right. Ivy covered most of the ship and tall palm trees had curved over the two-story upper deck cabins. The glass windows were broken with greenery growing around the rusted metal frames. From a distance, the boat completely blended with the jungle.

"Let's have a look inside." Turning on a flashlight on his phone, Ted entered a large crack in the hull. Dom and Jasmine stepped into the shadowy lower deck next, followed by Amy. Light leaked through numerous cracks and holes. There were plenty of dark crevices and cargo areas the light didn't reach. Amy's sandaled feet sank in a floor that had turned to wet mulch. The wood gave off a rotten mildew smell. White mold and a light green fur covered the plank walls that bowed around them. Ivy grew around the holes and cracks where sunlight glowed. Leafy roots veined parts of the interior walls. Wind moaned through the upper deck chambers and the wood creaked. Amy began to feel motion sickness as if they were at sea. The hull seemed to rock from side to side. She gripped a dangling iron chain to maintain her balance. The chain rattled and came crashing down beside her.

Everyone turned toward Amy.

"You okay?" Jasmine asked.

Amy nodded and took a deep breath to calm her pounding heart.

Ted's phone light illuminated fragments of wooden barrels that had long ago burst open.

"So much for drinking us some pirate's ale," Dom joked. Nobody laughed.

Ted opened a metal trunk full of trinkets and rusty tools. "These look modern." He pulled out a flashlight that didn't work, a fishing knife with a rubber handle, a pink thermos, a rusted metal tin with Polaroid photos, and a plastic doll with a rotted green face. Her body dripped mossy ooze. He tossed the doll and other contents back into the trunk.

Amy and Jasmine flipped through the small stack of Polaroids: a crew of eight Filipino men and women fishing on the double-decker boat...a happy group photo on a beach with a jungle background...various shots of them laughing and hiking through the jungle, eating mushrooms...posing in front of this ship.

Amy flipped one of the photos over and saw smeared writing on the back. "It's dated 1998."

"I wonder if they got off the island or if they were stranded here," Jasmine said. "And Dom, you better not make a pirate joke."

He held up his palms. "I'm wondering the same thing."

"Who knows?" Ted said. "I'm more interested in exploring the boat. This would make a great set piece for our movie."

Something rustled from one of the cabins a level above them.

"What the hell was that?" Jasmine asked.

Ted shined his light up to the ceiling. Several holes peered into a pitch-dark upper deck. The old vessel groaned as his light followed a staircase with broken stairs. "It's just the wind moving through the hull."

More rustling sounded from above, followed by a thump.

"That sounds like someone moving around up there," Amy said.

"Probably an animal or a bird roosting," Ted offered.

"Whatever it is, I've seen enough." Amy worked her way back through the shadowy hull and slippery mulch floor and stepped back outside. The other three followed her out. Jasmine looked equally spooked.

"Should we take a group-selfie in front the boat?" Dom asked.

"No," Amy and Jasmine said in unison.

Everyone remained silent as they hiked back through the jungle. Amy couldn't help wondering about who had explored the island before them. Were they the ones who had built the monkey hut? Or did the hermit kill them with his machete? She suddenly got the creepy thought that those hadn't been monkey skulls hanging in the hut, but shrunken human heads. As ridiculous as it sounded, Ted's theory of headhunters inhabiting this island began to feel like a real possibility. As branches and fern leaves constantly raked across her skin, Amy became wary of the jungle. She watched for any sign of movement. Every gloomy spot beneath the trees conjured images of natives with machetes. She knew these were just tricks of her mind, but for a moment the illusions seemed real enough to increase her pulse.

When they stepped back onto the beach of the first lagoon, she released a sigh of relief.

"I vote we get back on the boat," Amy suggested. "We probably need to get going to arrive back at the hotel by a decent hour."

"Didn't you tell her we're spending the night here?" Dom asked Jasmine.

"Um…" Jasmine bit her lower lip, as if caught in a lie.

Amy narrowed her eyes at her friend. "You said this was just a day trip."

"Our trip is for at least a couple days," Ted said. "Dom and I need to scout the rest of the island tomorrow and take photos, then check out some of the neighboring islands. You two ladies are our hostages until we decide to head back," he teased, rubbing her back.

Amy moved away from him.

Jasmine shrugged. "I figured once you got to the island, you'd want to stay a night or two."

"You know me better than that. I wish you'd given me a heads up before we left."

"You wouldn't have come."

"You're damn right I wouldn't have."

"Don't be mad," Jasmine pleaded.

Amy just gave her a hard stare. Jasmine averted her eyes.

Ted put his hands on Amy's shoulders and whispered in her ear. "Relax. We'll be sleeping on the boat tonight."

Not with you, I won't. Amy pulled loose from him and walked ahead of the others.

7

As the two men and two women returned to their picnic area on the beach, none of them realized they were being watched. Or that the salty scent of their skin could be smelled from the jungle. A curtain of vines parted to offer a view of the couples sitting down on their towels, their backs to the trees.

Their yacht floated gently in the lagoon. It was too far away for the visitors to see the slimy green footprints and bits of kelp that trailed from the back deck to the interior. Mossy handprints were smeared across the fridge and countertops. From the window of a bedroom below decks, the intruder watched the couples on the beach.

Amy rubbed goose bumps that had sprouted across her arms. "I can't shake the feeling we're not alone here."

"That marooned boat really got you spooked, eh?" Dom said.

"Doesn't it make you wonder what happened to the people who were on it?" Amy asked.

"Those photos were dated in '98," Ted said. "Those people are long gone by now."

"Or dead," Dom said, grinning. "Our monkey hunter hacked them all up with his machete."

"Ha, ha." Amy rolled her eyes.

Dom was getting on her nerves, and Ted kept touching her. The reserved gentleman who had been so polite and patient yesterday seemed to have gone, and this other Ted—all hands and leering gazes—had appeared in his place. And Dom, with his twinkle-eyed cuteness and joking around, seemed to be masking a side he didn't want the girls to see. It made her think of Carter Corelli. When Jasmine had first introduced him, Carter had been so polite, extremely handsome and charming, seemingly the perfect guy for her best friend to marry. He even had Amy fooled for a few months, until Carter began to show cracks in the nice-guy mask he wore. After he and Jasmine got married, he made several passes at Amy, which she shot down. But Carter was relentless. He even offered to pay her to sleep with him. "Come on, Amy, I know you're buried in debt. Let me pay off your student loans. All your credit cards. Help you start up that jewelry business, whatever you like. Just meet up with me a few times at the Four Seasons in Beverly Hills."

Amy had been stunned by the proposition. "What about Jasmine?"

"She never has to know."

Amy had gone straight to Jasmine and told her, but Carter denied it and spun the story around, accusing Amy of trying to seduce him to invest in her business. Jasmine, under his spell, had believed Carter and severed all communication with Amy. By the time Carter revealed what a snake he was, Jasmine had already endured four years of lies, brainwashing, and emotional abuse.

As Amy's stomach began to knot up again, she sensed similar Carter-like traits with Ted and Dom. She'd felt something off about them the moment their boat left the harbor this morning, a subtle shift in their personalities. Men who hid their true selves made her think of alligators and snakes, stealthy predators moving slowly toward their unsuspecting prey. Then, in a split second, before the quarry realizes it's too late, the predator strikes.

Amy studied Ted's and Dom's faces, trying to see what reptile lay beneath their facades. Dom looked away self-consciously. Ted interpreted Amy's watchful gaze as an invitation to rub her knee. He gave her his best charming smile, but all she saw was alligator teeth.

I can't believe we have to spend the night with these guys. Jasmine, I could kill you for tricking me. Why didn't I say no this morning? Why didn't I refuse to get on a boat with two strangers?

Because Jasmine would have gone with them anyway. Amy couldn't abandon her. She loved her sister more than any person on the planet and would do most anything for her, but sometimes Jasmine pushed Amy past her limits. She tried to signal Jasmine to go with her into the woods to talk in private. Amy wanted to express her concerns and urge her friend to sweet-talk Dom and Ted into taking them back. But Jasmine, already tipsy after her fourth beer, had her head turned, facing Dom.

The sun, high in the blue sky, blazed down on them. The balmy air shimmered like gasoline fumes over the lagoon and beach, making everyone sweat.

Jasmine fanned herself. "Damn, I'm burning up."

"Then take off your bathing suit," Dom said.

Without hesitation, Jasmine pulled off her bikini top. Her bare breasts attracted the gazes of both men. The male hormones in the air suddenly seemed palpable, radiating off their sweat-glistened muscles.

"There, don't you feel better?" Dom helped Jasmine apply suntan oil over her chest.

Amy felt uncomfortable. "Get a room."

Dom said, "We can check into the tiki hut up the beach."

Jasmine shuddered. "Ew, no way!"

"Feel free to take your top off too," Ted said, staring at Amy's breasts.

She crossed her hands over her bikini top. "Mine stays on."

Ted pouted. "Maybe later then. You think it's hot now, wait 'til the sun reaches its peak. By then, we all might want to strip down to our birthday suits."

The way Ted was leering at Amy, like he wasn't seeing *her*, just her body, like she was a living, breathing sex doll, caused a prickly sensation to creep across her back. This was going to be a long overnight trip.

To make matters worse, Jasmine said, "You're out of luck, Ted, Amy's a bit of a prude."

The comment stung. Memories over the years played out in her mind of Jasmine hooking up with guys and Amy shooting down their friends. *Is that really what I am? A prude?* Amy drank her beer, wondering why men's raw sexuality made her so edgy. She envied how Jasmine could feel so comfortable being sexually adventurous. For all the years they'd been friends, Jasmine had been a rebel willing to try anything. Amy figured it was partly due to Jasmine's strict upbringing. Her Filipino mother and American father, a Bible-thumping preacher, lived "according to the great gospel of Jesus Christ, our lord and savior," Jasmine liked to say in her father's voice. "And good girls wait 'til they're married before fornicating. Bad girls burn in Hell." Jasmine would never admit that her being a hedonist was her way of rebelling against her parents.

On the flip side, Amy's parents had been pot-smoking hippy artists who let Amy do whatever she pleased. No curfews, no lectures about sex, except to use protection. No rules about drugs, except stay away from meth and heroine. Most parents had cabinets filled with china. Her parents had a bong and glass pipe collection. On Amy's eighteenth birthday, she had tried smoking weed one time with her mom and dad. It had made her feel disconnected from her body, out of control, far from safe. Her parents had invited her to get high with them whenever she wanted. Ironically, Amy chose to go the conservative route and live drug-free. So when Dom and Ted pulled out a bag of drugs, Amy tensed up.

"It's time we take this party up a notch." Dom held up a little baggy of pink pills. "Who wants a hit of love candy?"

"I do." Jasmine opened her mouth, and Dom placed a tab of ecstasy on her tongue.

Ted popped an X pill into his mouth, then offered a pill to Amy. "Want to party?"

"I'll pass," she said.

"Sure?" Dom said, shaking his bag of multi-colored pills. "We've got plenty of candy. I've got coke, if you want to go high, or Xanax and Valium, if you'd prefer to go mellow. I've even got shrooms, if you'd rather get trippy."

"I'll stick with beer," Amy said.

"Amy doesn't do drugs," Jasmine said.

"Too bad, you're missing out." Dom popped a tab into his mouth.

Ted ran a finger along Amy's thigh. "How about you and I go back to the boat?"

"No. I'll stay right here."

Dom stood and pulled Jasmine to her feet. "Well, you kids have fun. The little lady and I are going to explore the island."

"No, Jasmine, don't go," Amy said frantically.

"Why not?" she challenged.

"Because...because..." *Because I don't want us to separate. I don't want to be alone with Ted, or you alone with Dom.* Amy tried to warn Jasmine with her eyes, but her friend was too drunk to pick up the signals. "I just think we should stick together."

"Well, I want some alone time with Dom."

"Then let's all go back to the boat," Amy said. "You two can have your privacy in one of the rooms. Ted and I will hang out upstairs."

"And do what?" Ted asked.

"I don't know, play cards or something."

Dom wrapped his arms around Jasmine from behind. "Me rather play Tarzan and Jane of the jungle."

Jasmine giggled like it was funny.

Amy walked after them and grabbed her wrist. "Seriously, Jazz. Don't go."

"Chill, sister, quit trying to control me." She pulled away and followed Dom into the trees.

Feeling hurt and scared, Amy called out, "Be careful and use your head. Don't wander too far."

"Yes, Mother. And you let loose for a change. You seriously need it."

"I'll make sure she has a good time." Ted slung his arm around Amy's shoulder and gave her a rough tug.

She felt a cramp in her gut as Jasmine and Dom disappeared in the woods, leaving her alone with Ted. His gaze rested on Amy's breasts again, and his tongue moistened his upper lip.

"Let's go for a swim." He tried to guide her toward the water.

Amy slipped loose. "Knock yourself out. I'm going to read the book I brought." She pulled a paperback novel out of her bag and sat down.

Ted marched toward the water, halted, then turned around. "You know, I'm getting the feeling you don't like me." The sharpness of his tone made Amy nervous.

"Sorry, I don't mean to be cold, but I don't know you well enough to act like we're on a date."

"Then get to know me." He stretched his arms wide. "I'm an open book. Ask me anything."

"Okay... Why did you get divorced four times?"

"Bad choices in women." He counted with his fingers. "Carla the cokehead, Sheila the gold digger, Simone the slut who slept with two of my friends, and Monica the nutcase who tried to run me over with her car."

"Wow, you really know how to pick 'em."

"I learned the hard way that you don't marry actresses. For too long I tried to be just like my father, but only recently realized I can't be him." His demeanor suddenly changed. He softened his eyes, his voice, gave her a wounded-boy look. "That's why I'm interested in getting to know *you*, Amy. You're not like typical women; you're real and deep, and you have an inner beauty that shines in your eyes."

"I also come with *a lot* of baggage."

"Don't we all." Calm now, he smiled and sat beside her. With his good looks and mysterious rich-boy charm, she could see why so many women would fall for his type. As Jasmine's wing girl, Amy had developed the ability to see through men's charms to their hidden motives. The trustworthy men, like Michael had been, were straight forward and authentic. They expressed their true feelings from the heart. You felt their love penetrate your soul. The devious men, the snakes and alligators who preyed upon women, flaunted their money, offered them drugs and alcohol to loosen inhibitions, used pick-up artist techniques like casual touching that escalated to putting their hand under a woman's clothes. And when those methods failed, they changed tack and flattered you and tried to win over your heart with sad stories. But since Ted began to show his true self, Amy could feel in her chest that his desire, which radiated like lava heat, was not coming from his heart. His words, whether truth or lies, were merely tactics to find a way to get inside her. Amy kept her guard up. She looked at him curiously.

He cocked his head, narrowed his eyes. "Why are you looking at me that way?"

"I'm just wondering…which wife gave you that scar across your nose?"

His eyes flared, and he looked away. He rubbed the bridge of his nose. "This was a gift from my mother. The Jacqueline Northcott you saw on TV was a total fake. In real life, she's a mean drunk."

"Oh, sorry."

He shrugged. "Not everyone gets lucky in the mom department."

From the pent-up rage that began radiating off Ted, Amy was afraid to explore any deeper. Normally, she was good at fending off men's advances, but she felt unsure about this one. She stopped drinking beer and switched to bottled water, deciding it was best to keep her senses sharp. While she kept her nose in her book, he pulled out a container of cocaine.

Using a rolled hundred-dollar bill, he snorted, wiped his nose. "Wants some blow?" He offered her the container of white powder, but she shook her head.

He wiped his sweaty brow. "Man, it's humid. Ready to go in for a skinny dip and cool off?"

Damn, he just won't give up.

"Not in the mood," she told him.

"No worries. We'll hang here then."

Oblivious to Amy's lack of interest, Ted kept talking, going on and on about his car and boat collection, his Malibu beach house, his condo in Aspen. His constant efforts to impress her were putting her through wing girl torture. She kept looking back at the jungle, wondering when Jasmine and Dom were going to return and save her from a death of boredom.

Ted finally got the hint that she'd stopped listening, and silence fell between them. He stared out at the water, brooding, his eyes intense like he was working out a strategy to get into her pants.

Amy had to pee in the worst way and was contemplating on whether to swim back to the boat to use the toilet or go into the forest. The yacht was about a sixty-yard swim. The jungle was just ten yards up the beach. *I don't think I can make it to the boat in time.*

Ted, now jacked up on coke, returned the beach towel next to her. The calculating look in his eyes made her think of Boyd Kuczek, a friend of her parents who had lived across the street. He had been in his mid-thirties and had curly brown hair and a beard. He and Amy's dad used to get stoned and talk politics. Sometimes Amy, a preteen at the time, had liked sitting with them. Boyd was a magazine photographer who had traveled all over South America. He told great stories about his adventures, like the time he visited a savage tribe in the Amazon rain forest and saw they were cooking up the bodies of their enemies. And the time he swam across a river teeming with crocodiles and piranhas. Boyd always grinned when he told stories, so Amy never knew if he was telling the truth or making it all up.

Whenever her dad stepped out of the room, Boyd looked at Amy in a funny way and made comments like "You're blossoming into a beautiful young woman." Amy had blushed because her chest was just beginning to form what her mom called breast buds.

One summer night, at one of their parties, while the adults got drunk and high on the back patio, Amy and Jasmine, both eleven, swam in the pool and played Marco Polo with Boyd Kuczek. He acted like an overgrown kid. When he caught them, he tickled the girls under the water and made them laugh. After the three of them got out and toweled off, Boyd invited Amy and Jasmine to see his collection of photographs. The girls were up past midnight, but Amy's parents were too high to care. Her mom was in the kitchen baking another batch of pot brownies. Her dad, taking a hit off a bong and passing it around a circle of friends, didn't notice Amy and Jasmine leave with Boyd.

Wrapped in towels, wet hair hanging past their shoulders, the giggling girls ran barefoot across the street and followed Boyd into his house. The den was decorated with tribal artifacts—wooden masks, goddess statues, ivory-carved totems, and animal skin rugs. Framed photographs of indigenous people living in jungle huts covered the walls. Jasmine elbowed Amy and pointed to pictures of native women with exposed breasts. The girls both giggled.

Boyd brought them glasses of red wine and told them, "In my house, you're old enough to drink." He winked and whispered, "It will be our little secret."

Amy and Jasmine thought it was cool that a grownup was treating them like adults. While they sipped their wine and pretended to be sophisticated ladies, Boyd pulled out his camera and asked the girls to pose for him. Amy felt self-conscious and shy, while Jasmine struck a few poses as Boyd circled them with his camera.

He told the girls they were pretty enough to be models. He complimented their bodies. Jasmine, who laughed nervously, was eating up the attention.

Boyd leered as he caressed each of them. Feeling icky from his touch, Amy wanted to go home. She was afraid to say so, because Boyd had a wild, scary look in his eyes, like he might hurt them if they made him mad.

Now, sitting on the beach, Ted wore a similar expression, a glassy-eyed leer that was a mix of drunken lust and predator. His hand pressed her wrist into the sand. He leaned toward Amy, going in for a kiss.

She stood fast, reminded how badly she had to pee. "Uh, nature calls. I'm going to go find a bush."

"I'll escort you."

"No, I can manage." Amy hiked into the woods to get far away from Ted. When it came to going to the toilet, she couldn't do it unless she was alone. Behind a bush, she pulled down her bikini bottoms and squatted to pee. She felt awkward doing it outdoors. Her bare rump brushed against prickly leaves. After a couple of beers, it took a while to empty her bladder.

Footsteps crunched through the jungle to her right. A silhouetted figure crouched in the shadows behind a clump of trees.

Her urine tract clamped midstream. "Ted, you better not be spying."

He didn't respond, just kept watching.

"I mean it, Ted. I need my privacy. Go the hell away!"

"You say something?" Ted called from a distance. She stood halfway up and saw through the limbs that he was still down at the beach, sitting on his towel.

Then who's watching me from the woods?

"Dom, Jasmine, is that you?"

The shadow stood. Too tall to be Jasmine. Too much growing on the head to be Dom. The head of the hiding figure moved into a ray of sun. It was covered in leafy camouflage.

An alarm went off inside Amy's head. *Someone else is on the island!*

She pulled up her bottoms and bolted back to the beach. She ran behind Ted and pointed. "There's someone back there."

"Who?"

"I couldn't tell. They were hiding in the brush, spying on me."

"Probably Dom. He likes to pull pranks when he's flipping on X."

Amy pictured Dom cloaked in leaves. That could have been a wig of vines dangling from his head. Had Jasmine been in on it too? She could be devious sometimes. *They're probably both laughing at my expense.*

Amy yelled, "Hardy har har, guys. If you're trying to scare me, mission accomplished."

"You can come out now," Ted called to them.

No one came forth.

"You sure it was Dom?" she asked Ted.

"Who else would it be?"

"The hermit who built that hut."

"Nonsense. We're as alone as alone gets." Ted stood behind her and massaged her shoulders. "You need to relax. All our teasing has gotten you spooked is all."

Amy nodded and sat back down on her towel. Her heart was still racing.

"You're really shaking. It's nothing a good buzz can't fix. Drink another cold one." Ted popped open two beers and offered her one.

"No thanks, I prefer to stay sober." Amy kept her eyes on the jungle.

8

The ecstasy had kicked in a while ago, giving Jasmine whole body tingles. Her heart was full of love now. She and Dom kept laughing over the silliest things, like her flip-flop getting stuck in the mud and him tripping over a vine. The sunlight brightened, and the forest turned greener. Myriad colorful flowers bloomed on the bushes and vines. She ran her fingers down a plant with hanging red flower bracts shaped like lobster claws.

"That's Heliconia," Dom said. "The pink ones next to them are oleander. I wouldn't touch them, though, they're highly toxic."

"You know about flowers?" Jasmine said.

"Don't act so surprised. I like to garden in my spare time. I have a greenhouse full of tropical plants. Over here is an orchid tree." Dom plucked a purple flower and stuck it behind her ear. "For my orchid queen of the jungle."

She wrapped her arms around his neck and gave him a kiss. "Didn't know you had a romantic side."

"There's a lot you don't know about me."

Deeper into the jungle, the foliage grew dense. There was no clear path. Dom and Jasmine had to weave around trees and vines and duck under branches. They crossed a freshwater spring that felt cool on her feet. The trickle was the only sound the forest made. Away from the water the jungle became eerily quiet. Every so often they passed the skeleton of a bird or scattered feathers.

"Strange that we don't hear any birds," Jasmine said. There wasn't a chirp of birdsong anywhere.

"I haven't seen a monkey or lemur either," Dom said. "Not even a lizard. These islands are usually teeming with animals. I bet the hermit ate them all."

She elbowed his ribs. "Don't bring up *him* again."

"The hermit's probably somewhere in this forest roasting the last parrot over a spit."

"I mean it, Dom." She kicked at his behind but missed.

He ran ahead, laughing. "You scare so easily."

"Asshole." Jasmine shook her head, but couldn't help smiling at how silly he looked stumbling through the bushes, trying to get away from her.

She liked Dom's quirky sense of humor. His fit body was eye candy too. She admired him as he hiked ahead of her, trailblazing through the jungle. *Him Tarzan, me Jane.* Sweat glistened his tanned muscles. She could bounce a quarter off his butt.

Dom wrestled with some branches. "I should have brought the machete, but I don't feel like going back for it."

The island seemed to go on forever. Nothing but trees and plants in all directions. Several times when they stopped, Jasmine had the impression that the jungle had sealed up behind them, concealing what little path they'd made. She felt disoriented. High, looming trees formed a canopy overhead. Ferns crowded the space.

"I don't think we should go any farther," she said. "I don't want to get lost."

"Just a few more yards. I see a clearing over there."

Through a stretch of gloomy woods, she spotted an area where bright sunlight broke through the trees. "Okay, but that's as far as we go."

"Check this out." Dom pointed to a dirty tennis shoe snared in a web of sticky vines. He pulled it a few times before it finally broke free. He held it up. "Our hermit's abandoned footwear." The shoe was covered in green lichen.

"That's a woman's shoe." Jasmine felt her nerves jump down her spine. "You said no one else was on the island."

"There's bound to have been plenty of explorers before us. Surely they're long gone by now." He tossed the shoe into the bushes. "Take my hand." He helped her jump across a ravine. They reached a clearing that had a grassy ground. The sun beamed hot on her shoulders.

"Hey, I think I spy something sweet to eat." Holding her hand, Dom led her to a crop of odd-looking trees covered in spirals of purple vines. The big-leafed branches were abundant with plump fruit that gave off a sweet scent. The skin of the fruits were dark purple with yellow spots.

"What kind of fruit are those?" Jasmine asked.

Dom pulled one off a branch. "Looks like papaya, but I've never seen this species." He broke it open, revealing a pink interior with purple seeds that burst instantly. Their tiny offspring floated in the air like dandelion. It looked like fairies were flying around her and Dom.

Jasmine laughed and spun in a circle. "Amazing."

He tasted the fruit first. "Jazz, you've got to try this."

He fed her the exotic fruit. Sweet juices dripped down her chin as she bit into the pulp. "Oh, my God, it's the best thing ever."

She and Dom continued to devour the fruit, sucking the juices. They scooped out pulp and fed it to one another.

"You feel that?" he asked, growing suddenly aroused. "It's like we're eating some kind of aphrodisiac."

"Oh yeah, I feel it." Jasmine's cheeks and chest began to heat up. Her nipples hardened. Her whole body tingled with an intense desire.

They began kissing feverishly. Dom picked her up, holding her in his arms and gazing into her eyes. A passionate heat burned between them. He laid her down on the soft bed of grass. They pulled off each other's bathing suits. In a field of floating purple dandelion, Dom and Jasmine melded into one.

Twenty feet away, a hand parted the branches, offering a view of the lovers. They seemed too oblivious to notice their watcher or the plants stirring in the jungle.

9

What's taking them so long? Amy wondered. A couple of hours had passed since Dom and Jasmine left. She was beyond worried. She couldn't shake the image of that shadow figure crouched in the bushes, their head and shoulders covered in ivy leaves.

It was just Dom trying to spook me.

What if it wasn't? You're in danger and you're ignoring your intuition.

No, I'm not. I'm stuck here because no one else wants to leave.

Unless whoever might be creeping through the forest showed himself, the others would remain convinced that Amy was afraid of an island bogeyman conjured from her fears.

The afternoon sun seemed to make the balmy air hotter and hotter. Amy walked to the water and waded knee deep to cool off. She also needed to get away from Ted. She'd had enough of fending off his advances. He was behaving like a douchebag who couldn't accept the word *no*.

She felt eyes boring into her, from the jungle, from the beach. A feeling of tiny spiders scurrying across her back made her shudder. Ted kept watching her, not even sneaking glances anymore. Staring at her like Boyd had on the night that changed her and Jasmine's lives.

Though she had worked with a therapist trying to recall and make peace with what happened that night, Amy only remembered bits and pieces. There was a lot of taking pictures and drinking wine. Then Boyd had suggested they play a game called "Natives."

"In the Amazon jungle," he'd told the girls, "natives don't wear any clothes, only paint. To them, it's natural to play naked together." He showed them a photograph of an Amazon man standing naked with two preteen girls. Their faces and bodies were decorated in red and black paint. Boyd pulled out a paint set and handed the girls some brushes. What happened after that was a blur, as if Amy's mind had blacked it out.

The last thing she remembered was her and Jasmine's faces and chests painted like natives… Boyd putting on a tribal mask of a green demon. He howled as he chased after them. Amy ran crying out of the house. She'd been so terrified that she'd gotten halfway across her lawn before realizing she'd abandoned her friend. Jasmine, screaming, tried to get away, but Boyd took hold of her arm and yanked her back into the house. The door slammed shut. Amy ran back and tried to open it, but he'd locked her friend inside.

Amy ran home and told her parents. They were so drunk and stoned that they had trouble following her story. Her mom couldn't get past that Amy was running around in just her bikini bottoms. Her dad cracked a joke about the tribal paint on her face. He thought she and Jasmine were playing some kind of game. When Amy cried and urged them to go help Jasmine, her dad went across the street and knocked on Boyd's door. Their neighbor wouldn't answer. All the lights were off.

"You sure she's in there, sweetie?" her dad asked impatiently.

"Yes, Boyd won't let her out," Amy said.

"Jasmine can be a little devil when she wants to be. Maybe she went back to the house. Come on." Amy's dad took her hand and walked her back to their house.

Of course, they didn't find Jasmine there. Amy begged her mom and dad to call the police. Her parents debated on what to do because they had a house full of pot and were paranoid by nature. They tried to rationalize that maybe Amy had misunderstood Boyd. They couldn't believe their friend would do anything to the harm the girls; so they assumed it was Amy and Jasmine who were misbehaving. "I wouldn't put it past Jasmine to talk you into painting yourselves like that," Amy's dad said. "I'm sure you're overreacting."

While her parents discussed what to do, Amy called 911. The police finally came and broke down the door to Boyd's house. An officer carried Jasmine out wrapped in a blanket. She had been in complete shock.

After the incident, Amy spent time in therapy. She had completely shut down and developed a thick armor. She had been celibate as a nun through high school and most of college. When she finally opened her heart to Michael, the man she eventually got engaged to, she'd dated him for months before sleeping with him. Michael's untimely death had left Amy vulnerable and needing Jasmine more than ever.

Through yoga and kickboxing and self-help retreats, Amy had spent years trying to exorcise Boyd Kuczek out of her mind. But he was always there, lurking in the shadows.

When the police had brought out the pedophile handcuffed, and again during his trial, Boyd had leered at Amy with a look that would gleam in the eyes of many men to come. Now, Ted's intense stare made her skin prickle. Any minute now she expected him to slip off his swimsuit and ask her to play Natives.

Amy looked back at the jungle. *Jasmine and Dom, please come back.*

After shuddering with uncontrollable ecstasy, Jasmine collapsed on top of Dom's chest. She lay in his arms until the orgasmic contractions took her into a state of bliss.

"Damn…" she whispered, giggling.

He laughed with her, his chest vibrating her, sending off a few more seismic waves of pleasure.

She stroked his arm. "I'm so glad I met you, Dom."

"Same here."

"It's been years since I felt this happy. My ex-husband totally neglected me."

"He must have been a real tool to let you go. You're an amazing woman, Jasmine."

"Thanks, you don't know how much I needed to hear that. I'm still recovering from the hell Carter put me through."

"I'm sorry he mistreated you."

"When we got married, I thought I'd found the perfect guy for me. He really had me fooled. He somehow convinced me to cut everyone out my life that I loved, my parents, all my friends. I swear I married the Devil."

Dom stroked her head. "Not all men are bad. Some of us want nothing more than to make our woman happy."

"Thank God there are men like you. What hurts most is that I didn't see the lie that my marriage was. Divorce is the worst. I've never felt such heartbreak and anger and confusion."

"You get over it, eventually," Dom said. "My ex-wife and I had our own bitter divorce. We even had a custody battle over our daughters."

Jasmine leaned up on one elbow. "I didn't know you children."

"Ages four and six. Libby and Grace." His whole face lit up when he said their names. "They're the most important things in the world to me."

"Did you win custody?"

"My wife and I ended up settling for the sake of the girls. They live with their momma during the week. I get them every other weekend and two full weeks in the summer."

"I bet you're a good dad."

"Try to be. Raising girls is tough. Half the time they're raising me. Do you ever plan to have kids?"

"Someday. I've got to get my life straightened out first."

He rolled onto his side and caressed her back. "Anything I can do to help with that?"

"Mmm-hmm, keep doing that." The way he touched her was better than a massage at the spa.

"I really like you," he said softly.

"I'm sure you say that to *all* the girls."

"I only say it when I mean it, Jazz. I like you. I could easily see us dating back in L.A."

"Please, don't go getting sentimental on me. Right now, I need this to just be a fling, nothing complicated."

"I'm not asking you to marry me, my orchid queen." He kissed her shoulder. "But the fireworks we just made…" Gentle kisses moved to her neck, getting her hot again. He whispered into her ear, "I'd like to do it a dozen more times…"

Kissing Dom's lips, Jasmine pulled him on top of her.

10

Dom got the nympho and I'm stuck here with Sandra fucking Dee.

Ted was getting nowhere with Amy. The bitch was giving him major blue balls. He wasn't used to women rejecting him. Not after he took them shopping, wined and dined them, and gave them a ride on a yacht. The actresses he worked with put out easily. He was usually balls deep by now. What the fuck was Amy's problem? Was she a lesbian? No, she didn't fit the type. Just a damn prude. Or a gold-digging user like his second ex-wife. Amy was going to milk all the gifts she could get out of him without returning any favors. He hated women who used men. His mother was like that. Used his father to get roles in movies and TV shows, then when she was a star, she divorced him and took half of his fortune.

"Your mother's no different than a whore," his father told Ted when he was ten. "She uses her body to get what she wants, and after she's taken all she can from you, she turns into an ice-cold bitch. Stay away from women like your mother, Ted, they'll suck you dry."

His father's words had confused Ted, because as a boy he had worshipped his mother like a goddess—a tall, blonde, green-eyed Venus. She had started out as a model. There were large framed photographs of her all around the house—Mother posing evocatively for the camera, wearing exotic makeup and sexy clothes that exposed a lot of skin. He had been most fascinated with a black and white nude photo of Mother that hung in her closet. Ted had loved the way she walked around the house in her silk nighties that exposed her long legs and the cleavage of her cosmetically perfect breasts. He'd loved the way she showed him affection after a few martinis. Sometimes, when she had gotten drunk and needy, she'd let little Ted lay in bed with her, and he'd get aroused, because her breasts were right there, pressing into his cheek. She called it their "cuddle time." This went on for a few years, until Ted hit puberty, then suddenly Mother acted repulsed by him. When he tried to crawl into bed with her and do more than just cuddling, she pushed him way, said he was sick, "Mothers and sons don't do *that*!" But Ted, all hormones and animal lust, took what he had wanted from her anyway. Because Father was right. Mother was a whore.

When Amy walked down to the water to cool her feet, Ted snorted some more Filipino blow that shot bolts of lightning behind his eyes. The adrenaline was like Viagra. A blood-pumping hard-on and blue balls were a painful combination.

Amy walked back up the beach, hugging herself. Her body in that bikini was driving him wild.

"Come here." Ted held out his hand. "Let's dance."

She looked at him like he was nuts. "There's no music."

"We'll make our own."

"I think we should go look for Dom and Jasmine."

"Forget about them. Let's lay down together." He stepped toward her. "I'll give you a back rub."

She backed away. "Don't touch me."

"Damn it, I'm tired of you giving me mixed signals."

"Let me be *very clear*, Ted. You and me…it's not going to happen. Not now, not tonight, not ever."

"Fucking cocktease. You sure haven't minded prancing around in that bikini I bought you."

"You can have it back later."

"I want it right now. Take it off."

"You're fucked up and you're scaring me. Please, Ted, back off."

He grabbed her arm and pulled her against him. "Stop playing hard to get." He slid his hand inside her bikini and groped her breast.

"Stop it!" Amy clawed his face.

His eye and cheek burned from the gashes. In a flash Ted saw his drunk mother lying naked on the bed, angry and shocked. She yelled, *You're a sick boy, Teddy, doing that to your mother!* His body shook with shame. Mother screamed, *Get out of my room! Get out!* He watched helplessly as Mother hurled her martini at him. He felt the glass shatter across his face. Blood ran into his eyes. Then everything went blurry.

Ted growled and lashed out. The back of his hand connected with something solid. He heard a thud. Next thing he knew, Amy was lying face down on the ground.

He wiped blood off his burning cheek. "Fucking bitch, look what you've done."

She didn't move. He rolled her over. Amy was lights out.

11

While Jasmine napped in the grass, Dom watched her sleep. He'd only known her since yesterday, but he was already developing feelings for her. When he first met her at the hotel's pool, he had been curiously drawn to her, not just because she was pretty either. Jasmine had a spark in her jade green eyes and an aura that had made him desire to meet her.

Dom had feared that too many years working with shallow people in the film business had desensitized him. He couldn't remember the last time he'd had a deep connection with a woman. He'd felt nothing for the actresses and models he'd slept with since his divorce. Their Barbie doll faces and bodies all blurred together. None of his recent relationships had lasted more than a couple of months, and those had been more superficial than loving. His existence of constant partying with booze, drugs, and sex had become shallow and devoid of meaning. Now that he had met a woman who seemed like a kindred spirit, Dom felt himself going into a strange new place. Being intimate with Jasmine seemed to be bringing all of his feelings to the surface. His heart being vulnerable scared him, but he liked the warm sensation coursing through him, the desire to explore more intimacy with Jasmine.

There's more to me than being a prankster and a lover, he wanted to tell her. But it was way too soon to start getting sappy. Recently divorced and treating him as just someone to have a good time with, Jasmine clearly had her own defenses to letting a man into her heart. He'd have to take things slow with her.

Dom caressed her hair. Jasmine purred, but kept her eyes closed. He whispered, "Be right back, Sleeping Beauty," and kissed her forehead.

He walked twenty yards away and took a leak, humming as he sprayed an ivy-covered tree. Just beyond a thatch of fruit and orchid trees was another sunlit clearing. A bird with a yellow breast and green wings flew down into a patch of purple vines. It was the first *live* bird he'd seen since entering the island. Its singular chirping sounded strange against the otherwise silent jungle. Dom finished his business, then stepped through the woods for a closer look. The exotic bird hopped along the ground, pecking for seeds. The plants around it started to move like a den of snakes. A purple pod the size of a fist rose on a stalk. The pod slowly opened, revealing a pink mouth with long needles. In a viper's snap, the plant's jaws clamped around the bird. It flapped its wings inside the cage of teeth. Saliva dripped onto the feathers, burning through them like acid, and the bird chirped louder.

Dom watched in awe as the plant's pod crushed the bird, squirting out its blood. Other stalks moved in and made slurping sounds as they drank the red droplets.

What the hell kind of plants are those? If they were a species of Venus flytraps, they were the biggest he'd ever seen. Dom shook his head, disbelieving. The jungle around him suddenly became noisy with chittering sounds. All the trees and bushes in the clearing began to shake. In a bush beside him, flowers opened, emitting a sweet floral musk. When it struck Dom's nose, he became instantly paralyzed. He stood frozen, his arms hanging helpless at his sides, his feet rooted to the ground. His neck muscles locked. *Fuck, what's going on? Why can't I move?* His heartbeat quickened as a wave of panic surged through him. Something crawled over his feet. Suddenly, he was standing ankle-deep in a cluster of slithering purple vines. A dozen more needle-toothed pods rose their heads like snakes.

"Oh, shit!" Dom tried to back away, but his body remained a rigid statue in a garden of evil. His skin still felt every slithering-crawling sensation as the leafy vines weaved around his legs and wrapped around his torso and arms. Footsteps approached from behind.

"Jasmine, is that you?" his words came out as a tearful plea. "Help me…"

A tall bush writhed against Dom's back. Two green skeletal hands appeared from behind and clutched his arms, pulling Dom into a tight embrace. A bony jaw pressed against his cheek and moved as it made a clucking sound. A spiky tongue licked his face and scraped off a layer of skin.

Dom cried out, unable to run or fight. The bush-thing released its hands and backed away. The tangle of leafy ropes constricted around Dom's legs, waist, and chest, squeezing so tight he struggled to breathe. Out of the corner of his eye, something lowered from a tree. His head turned to see a tall pink orchid, dripping with golden sap. Its petals fanned open beside his face. Rows of sharp teeth spiraled inside the flower's lamprey mouth.

Dom screamed.

The orchid latched itself onto his face.

As Jasmine lay in the sun in a state of bliss, leaves tickled her toes and the bottoms of her feet. She giggled. "Dom, what are you doing?"

Then something bit her toes. "Ouch!"

She sat up.

Purple vines with pods had unraveled from the fruit trees and crept across the grass. They draped a sticky, leafy blanket over her lower legs. At the center of the vines kneeled a green child-sized creature covered head to toe in ivy and moss. The thing croaked at Jasmine, exposing a mouth full of green needle-sharp teeth. The thing lurched and clamped its mouth onto her right foot, sending a fiery venom-like sensation into her bloodstream. Screaming, Jasmine kicked the creature's head, ripping her foot loose from its clutches. She backed away. Her sliced-up toes bled heavily. The blanket of vines and pods fought to slurp the blood off the ground. Other vines squirmed toward her bloody foot.

She scooted farther away from the rising stalks. Their pod heads with chomping jaws made high-pitched sounds like singing cicadas. At the center of the writhing green mass, the child-sized creature stretched out its skeletal arms as if wanting a hug.

Jasmine screamed for Dom. He shouted a distance behind her. She got to her feet and ran-limped to his cries of terror and pain. He lay on the ground at the center of another squirming bed of plants. Creeping purple vines wrapped around his arms and legs. Dozens of pods and flowers with sharp teeth bit into him. Blood covered the tendrils around his body. The skin of Dom's face had been flayed off, leaving a red mask with wide, pleading eyes. "Help!"

Jasmine grabbed his hand and pulled. The plants coiled tighter around him. A thick vine strangled his neck like a noose. He made choking sounds. His eyes bulged. A pod with a viper-sized jaw bit into his throat. Blood sprayed Jasmine's chest.

Dom stopped screaming. The flowery tentacles covered his entire body, eating his skin to bone.

Jasmine put a hand over her mouth. She backed away, shaking to the core. Behind her, the small creature in the second patch of vines creeped on hands and knees toward her. Beyond it, a tall, bushy, leaf-cloaked figure appeared in the jungle. The thing stood erect like a man on two legs, but walked hunched over as it moved through the shadows. Bony arms hung at its sides. A jungle of ferns and ivy grew out of its back. Roots hung from its head like dreadlocks. A clucking sound issued from its throat. The small creature mimicked the tall one. All around, the carnivorous plants chittered with the bush people.

Crying, Jasmine turned to run.

12

Amy woke to a sight of palm trees spinning around blue sky. Hot sun on her face. Warm sand beneath her back. She felt woozy. The left side of her jaw ached. She rubbed her bruised cheek, her cut lip. *The motherfucker hit me.*

Ted was pacing down by the water, cursing and talking to himself. "You did it again! No, the bitch made me do it. She made me do it!"

Amy sat up, adjusted her bikini top to cover her breasts. Both were sore and with red blotches, especially around the nipples. *Did this creep grope me while I was out cold?*

Ted's back was to her. He squatted and beat his fists against his head. An enraged ape. "Fucking idiot!"

She had to get away from this lunatic. She needed to find Jasmine and Dom. Amy got to her feet and crept toward the jungle.

Ted turned around. "You're awake."

Amy paused for a second, locking eyes with him.

"Look what you did to me." He pointed to the bloody scratch marks down one side of his face.

"You wouldn't stop."

"Where do you think you're going?"

"Stay the fuck away from me!" She hurried toward the forest.

"Get back here!" He charged and grabbed her wrist.

Amy spun and kicked him in the groin. Ted doubled over and fell to the ground.

She took off into the jungle, searching for Jasmine.

Which way back to the beach? Jasmine struggled through a shadowy forest that offered no clear direction. Every branch and bramble scraped her skin. Every exposed root tripped her. Thick brown vines hung from the trees. Fat elephant-ear leaves blocked nearly every way she turned. Pushing blindly through the leaves, she limped, favoring her left foot. Where she'd been bitten, Jasmine felt needles of pain every time she put weight on her right foot.

She still couldn't believe Dom was dead. *That writhing mass of plants had eaten him.* His blood speckled her chest and bikini. Tears trickled down her cheeks.

The wind blowing against her carried the smell of salt water. The lagoon had to be up ahead. She called for help over and over, hoping Amy and Ted would hear her. Jasmine yelled until her voice went hoarse. When no one responded, a horrid thought came to mind: *What if I'm going the wrong way?*

She imagined wandering to the opposite side of the island, to a deserted beach where another hut stood. Only this one was occupied by a plant-man covered in vines. And when it spoke, its throat clicked like the wings of a cicada.

The image made Jasmine move faster. She stepped around a wide tree and bumped into Ted's chest.

"Thank God," she said, hugging him.

He grabbed her shoulders and held her away from him. His eyes looked deranged, his pupils dilated. "Where's Dom?"

Jasmine teared up again and pointed behind her.

Ted looked down at her bloody bikini. "What the hell happened?"

"He's de… Dom's dead."

"What the fuck did you do?"

"Not me…" She tried to explain, but she could barely speak through her sobs.

Ted pulled her arm hard, as if trying to yank it from her socket. "Take me to him."

Jasmine struggled to break free from his painful grip, but his strength outmatched hers. He yanked her and shook her until she finally gave up trying to escape. Recognizing the stream she'd crossed earlier, she led him back the way she'd come.

She found the clearing where she'd left Dom. The bed of carnivorous plants and bush people were gone. Dom's body nowhere to be found. The only sign he'd been there was a long blood stain on the grass.

"Where is he?" Ted asked.

"I left him right there."

Ted knelt and ran his fingers through the blood. Then he looked at Jasmine with crazed eyes. "You killed him?"

"No."

"Then explain why there's so much blood."

"The plants…ate him."

"Bullshit. You murdered my friend, you fucking little bitch."

She shook her head, backing away.

Ted lunged and gripped her throat, choking her. Jasmine fought to breathe. His fingers squeezed tighter, digging deeper into her neck. Her eyes watered. She stared up at blue sky ringed by palm trees.

She heard a loud smack, and Ted collapsed. She fell to the ground with him.

Amy stood above them, gripping a log.

13

"It's going to be okay." Amy held Jasmine crying against her shoulder. Still gripping the log, she watched Ted to make sure he didn't get back up. She'd smacked him hard enough to crack his skull. A patch of blood stained the back of his head. *Served him right, the fucker.*

Was he dead? She couldn't tell. Ted lay face down near the edge of the trees. Dangling fern branches hid half of his body.

Jasmine explained what happened to Dom. The news of his death hit Amy like a punch to the gut. She found her friend's story about flowers with teeth impossible to believe. There were no killer plants in sight. The jungle surrounding the clearing remained quiet and still. Jasmine must have hallucinated the plants attacking, appearing shaped like bony people. The ecstasy she'd taken could have been laced with acid, or Dom sprinkled powder into her beer. Amy wouldn't put it past these assholes to secretly drug them. Ted certainly seemed the type to roofie his dates who didn't give him what he wanted. She could still feel his fingers on her breasts, the sore spots where he'd groped and pinched while she'd been unconscious. Sick fucker. Amy had half a mind to go over and bash his skull in. She stopped herself from acting on her anger. The first blow had been self-defense. She'd saved Jasmine from being strangled. Any more blows to Ted's head would take Amy to a murderous place she didn't want to go.

The possibility that Jasmine might have been drugged with a hallucinogen made Amy wonder if she could believe any of her story. Was Dom really dead? Without a body, she couldn't be sure. There was no denying all the blood on the ground. Jasmine had only a cut foot, so it had to be his. What had really happened? *Did Dom attack her like Ted did me?* Now was not the time to grill Jasmine.

We've got to figure out what to do next.

The two men who'd brought them here, who knew how to drive the yacht, who knew how to find their way out of this maze of islands, were either dead or dangerous.

And if Dom turns up alive and Ted wakes up...

Amy tried not to think about it. One issue at a time.

She couldn't fathom how she and Jasmine were going to operate the yacht and make it all the way back to Manila on their own. Nor could she ever trust Ted enough to get back on the boat with him. *We are so fucked.* Tears formed but Amy held them back. *No, there's a way out of this. Jasmine and I will figure a way out.* Their first challenge was finding the lagoon and getting off this island.

Amy wiped Jasmine's tears. "Let's make our way back to the boat."

"What about the keys? Ted locked up the boat. He put the keys in his pocket."

Amy cursed and looked back at his prone body. "I'll get them."

She crept toward him, the log in her hand raised ready to strike. *Make one move, motherfucker, and your skull is pulp.*

He remained on his stomach, head facing toward the fern branches. His long bathing suit had several zipper pockets. She felt the two pockets on the side closest to her. Both empty. Nothing stored in the back pockets either except a roll of lip balm. Shit, she was going to have to turn him over to reach the opposite side.

She held out the log to Jasmine. "Hold this. Be ready to hit him if he tries anything."

Amy then gripped Ted's far hip with both hands and rolled him onto his side. She felt a lump in the bottom pocket and heard a chink of metal. She unzipped the pocket and clutched a spongy foam keychain. "Got it." She pulled the keys out.

Ted's hand clutched her wrist. He growled as he tried to sit up. The grass and fern branches had attached themselves to his face and one side of his body. Moving like feelers, the plants wormed their way into his skin.

Amy's mind denied what she was seeing—so much blood leaking out of Ted and onto patches of long, tube-shaped grass that swayed hungrily like sea anemone toward a snared fish. The plants dug deeper into the holes of Ted's face and ribs. The green tubes swelled as they sucked blood from him. Vines of ivy joined in on the feast, taking hold of his leg.

Crying out, Ted pulled Amy toward him, toward the green tentacles searching for new flesh to attach to. His growls turned to cries of agony. The plants made slurping sounds as they *drank* him.

Amy fought to pull away, but Ted wouldn't let go of her wrist.

Jasmine struck his arm with the log. His grip released, and Amy fell back on her rump. She dropped the keys halfway between her and Ted. He reached for the keys. Jasmine hammered his hand like she was trying kill a spider with a bat.

Amy snatched the keys and backed away, pulling Jasmine with her.

Ted tried to stand but the plants had him completely ensnared. Several branches, flower-dotted vines, and grass tubes took hold of him. The torn skin along his chest and ribs exposed the red layer beneath.

"Help!" he pleaded.

The girls kept a safe distance and watched the horror show of Ted being eaten alive. The plants slurping and crunching as they drank and gnawed. The whole jungle seemed to come alive. The bushes around him shook violently. The trees set farther back made cracking sounds as they waved their branches. High up in a tree, a skeletal man covered in plants clucked his tongue. A second leaf-covered figure, this one smaller, the size of a child, clucked from the base of the tree. The nightmarish vision made Amy wonder if she was hallucinating. This couldn't be happening.

A large vine, thick as a boa constrictor, slid out of the ferns and wrapped around Ted's waist. The vine yanked him into the bushes. In a blink, he was gone.

14

Thunder rumbled. Amy looked up at the darkening sky. Storm clouds had rolled in. *We have to find the lagoon before nightfall.* With arms around each other's shoulders, Amy helped Jasmine hike through the jungle. Jasmine held her injured foot off the ground as she hopped on her other leg.

The gray gloom beneath the branch canopy grew darker. Every plant they passed posed a potential threat. Any wrong path could lead through a gauntlet of bloodsucking meat eaters. A grove of green elephant ears swayed as they passed. Closed flowers chirped like night crickets. Amy and Jasmine stayed to the center of the thin path, avoiding every plant and root they could. It was impossible not to brush up against branches and bushes, though. Every step was a risk.

"You okay?" Amy asked.

Jasmine whimpered. "My foot hurts bad. And Dom…" She gave out a choked sob.

"I know," Amy said, holding her friend close. The whole afternoon seemed like a fevered dream, too horrible to be real.

They crossed through an overgrown thicket where branches intertwined. As they wove between moss-covered trees, Amy's mind couldn't shake the image of that leafy-green figure perched up in the tree, and the smaller one at the base. They had been camouflaged against a trunk covered in ivy. Had the shapes not moved and made clucking sounds, Amy might not have spotted them. She kept looking up to make sure the things weren't following them through the branches.

They weren't real, her logical mind tried to convince her. *And the plants didn't attack Dom or Ted.*

Amy knew how powerful hallucinating drugs could be. In college, while attending a frat party, a guy had secretly slipped something into Amy's drink that made her feel strange. Shortly after, the floor had teetered and the walls stretched. The party became a wonderland of colors and laughing cartoon characters. Everything took on a watery texture and kept morphing like a dream. In the bathroom, the wallpaper had formed faces that talked to her. Her hallucinations had seemed so real. As much as Amy wanted to believe she'd been drugged by Ted and had imagined the jungle attacking him, drinking his blood, Amy felt sober, her senses heightened by fear. She snapped her head toward every crackling sound, every twitching leaf.

Jasmine leaned on Amy's shoulder as they continued to feel their way through the jungle. They needed to get back to the boat. If Ted was still alive, there was no telling what he would do to them.

Rain sprinkled, making pitter-patter sounds on the leaves. Then it came down in heavy wet blasts, soaking the girls from head to toe. They shivered as they held onto one another. Cracks of lightning flashed overhead. At last, Amy spotted the beach through the trees. She and Jasmine stepped onto the damp sand. The yacht bobbed on the lagoon's choppy water. Hours ago, the swim from the boat to the beach was a cinch. Now, in the rain, the dark pool looked eager to drown them.

"Think you can swim?" Amy asked.

Jasmine shook her head. "Not with this leg."

Amy knelt in the rain and examined Jasmine's leg. Her foot and calf had swollen as though bitten by a venomous snake. Her sliced big toe had turned purple and looked like a plum oozing pus. Amy needed to get Jasmine to the boat to clean and dress that wound.

"I can swim backward with you on my chest."

"You haven't been a lifeguard since high school," Jasmine said.

"I've still got the skills." Amy had rescued a few people at the beach, but never in a storm.

Jasmine looked uncertain. "All right."

They started into the water. Jasmine screamed. "It burns! It burns! I can't do it." The salt water was too painful for the open cut, so Amy helped her back onto the beach.

The storm escalated into a monsoon. Palm trees bent in the wind. Gusts of cold rain whipped Amy and Jasmine sideways.

"We have to find shelter!" Amy yelled.

There was only one option, and neither of them liked it.

15

Ted went in and out of consciousness. He was faintly aware of a burning pain, like fire ants stinging his feet. Mostly he felt numb below the neck. Rainwater slapped the leaves, dripped onto his face.

Where am I? Dead? No, I can feel my lungs struggling to breathe.

His eyelids slowly opened. The sunny afternoon had darkened. A storm shook the treetops. Streamers of rain fell down. Strange trees circled around him. He'd seen this exotic species in other tropical locations, Hawaii and Thailand. What were they called? His mind searched for the name...*Bodhi trees!* Their trunks were several feet wide with dozens of exposed roots that reminded him of octopus tentacles. The Bodhi trees loomed high above him. Thick, bushy branches blocked out most of the sky, except for a small ring of gray light. He counted six ancient trees in all, their roots intertwined, including the Bodhi he was bound to. Its smaller roots had wrapped around his chest and legs, fettered his wrists and ankles.

Something moved off to Ted's right. A red skeletal man was tied by roots to another tree. Despite the skull face, Ted recognized his friend—dark hair still covered Dom's scalp. The rest of him had been skinned, exposing bloody sinew and bone beneath.

Oh, God, what did they do to you?

Dom's eye sockets were empty cavities. His nose and lips were gone. His visible teeth and gums looked like a grim smile. Somehow, Dom wasn't dead. Not quite. His jaw moved. His hands twitched. Slithering vines burrowed through holes in his muscles, wrapped around his bones.

The plants…they're what's keeping Dom alive, animating him like the strings of a puppet.

This island was like some lush green version of hell.

And we're its captives.

Numbness faded away. Ted's awareness of fire ant stings returned. The pain rose up his legs to his torso, neck, and face. He had the sensation of ants crawling all over him. Yet his hands, fixed to the tree, couldn't swat the bugs away.

He looked down. His clothes had been ravaged. Every area of exposed flesh was covered not in ants, but green lichen. Together, the moving fungus and algae were eating through his skin, working their way into his muscles like a rampant green cancer. He could see part of his knee bone, the metatarsals and phalanges of his feet. Wide awake now, he screamed for the torturous pain to stop.

A bush at the center of the circle started to move. As it stood to face him, Ted realized in horror it was not a bush, but a skeletal man cloaked in ivy, fungus, and other varieties of fauna. The island's hermit. The builder of the monkey hut. Green and purple vines weaved up and down his bones and through his ribcage like arteries. The hermit didn't appear to be a living man. The jungle must have taken his life long ago. What gray flesh was left had rotted. But the man's corpse was alive, thanks to the colonies of plants living on him and festering inside him. He—*it*—seemed to have an awareness. The hermit studied Ted for a long moment, head cocked to one side.

Terror and excruciating pain drove Ted mad as he wailed. The hermit's bony hand gripped his jaw. Its skull drew within inches of his face. Tucked inside its left eye socket, like a hermit crab, was a prickly pod. Its sharp-toothed jaws slowly opened like a Venus flytrap's. Then the stalk shot out, and the pod's mouth clamped onto Ted's right eye. He screamed as it plucked the orb from its socket.

As if Hell had mercy, the numbness returned. He floated in a euphoric state of complete surrender.

Small roots from the Bodhi trees branched over Ted's and Dom's faces and dug into their ears. Their bodies tremored as they fused with the ancient trees.

PART TWO

Night Stalkers

16

Constant rain thumped against the hut's thatch roof. A damp spray blew into the front opening where there was no wall. The hanging strings of monkey skulls knocked together as they swayed in the wind.

Amy had gotten Jasmine seated at the back of the shack. She'd then run down the beach to fetch the waterproof beach bag and some leftover sandwiches and water bottles from the cooler. The bag contained one dry towel and a white cotton shirt. Amy gave them both to Jasmine, wrapping the towel around her shoulders. They ate soggy sandwiches, while the tropical storm outside thrashed the island and shook the hut. Amy feared that at any second the wind would snatch to roof away and toss them back into the jungle.

"We have to figure out a way to get you on that boat," Amy told her. "I need to treat that wound." The dark purple around her friend's big toe had spread to cover her entire foot.

"I can't get in that water. I'm screwed." Jasmine looked on the verge of giving up. "Maybe you should leave me and take the boat."

"There's no way I'm leaving you behind. We're getting off this island together, sister."

Jasmine sniffled and nodded. "I'm sorry."

"What for?"

"It's my fault we're in this mess. We should never have come on this trip."

"Stop blaming yourself. I agreed to come along."

"But I pressured you to join us. I knew you'd agree to if I pleaded hard enough. You always do."

"You calling me a pushover?"

"No, but you're willing to sacrifice yourself for others. I took advantage of that. I was only thinking about me having fun with Dom. I'm sorry I asked you to entertain Ted."

Amy put a hand on her shoulder. "You're forgiven. Now, let's put that behind us and figure out a plan." As they sat there quiet, listening to the storm, an idea came to Amy. "I just remembered, there's a dinghy stored at the back of the boat. I can go get it and come back for you."

"That water looks too risky. I don't want you to drown."

"Don't worry about me, Jazzy. I'm a fish in the water." Amy stood, excited about her new plan. It gave her hope. *Yes, get my girl to the boat, dress that foot, call for help, and figure out a way to power up the yacht.* They didn't have to navigate all the way back to Manila. Just drive the boat out of the lagoon and radio for help.

Amy told Jasmine her plan and gripped her hands. "We can do this. We're going to survive." She got up to leave.

"I'm afraid to be alone out here."

"Ted won't be bothering us anymore."

"What about those walking bush things?" Jasmine asked.

Amy had forgotten about them. The more the two had shared what they'd witnessed, the more Amy believed the figures covered in vines were real. She'd only glimpsed what might have been the tall one while she'd squatted to pee in the woods, and later when she'd spotted its camouflaged shape up on a tree branch, along with the smaller figure at the base.

"At first, I thought they were jungle people wearing vines, but I don't think they were human."

"What else could they be?" Amy asked.

Jasmine shrugged. "The short one bit my foot."

Even though they had safely gotten away from the carnivorous plants, they didn't feel safe. The monkey headhunter who'd built this hut could return.

Amy picked up the rusty machete they'd found earlier and handed it to Jasmine. "If anyone comes into the hut that's not me, you split their skull."

17

As twilight receded, a full moon occasionally broke through the clouds. The angry storm still pummeled the island. The white boat bobbed in the waves. Had it drifted farther from the shore? On a calm day that distance would take Amy less than a minute. In that rough chop she would have go into champ mode, just like she did when she raced heats for her high school swim team.

Amy waded into the cold water. The seaweed forest beneath the surface seemed to have grown thicker. Leafy branches swayed against her legs as she reached waist deep. One of the stalks snared her ankle. It stopped her progress, tethering her to the sandy bottom. Another slimy strand wrapped around her wrist.

"What the fuck?"

She fought to pull herself free. All around her little islands of kelp rose out of the water, drifting toward her.

She jumped backward, kicking with both feet, and broke free of the stalks. The icy water shocked all her nerves as she spun around and swam freestyle. Hard rain pelted her back. With each gulp for air, her mouth took in salt water as choppy waves splashed her face. More kelp tendrils grazed her belly and thighs as she glided over the surface. She kicked too fast for the seaweed to take hold.

Forty yards from the boat, she switched to breaststrokes. Her mind focused on one stroke at a time and keeping the yacht's silhouette in her line of sight. She reached the swim platform at the stern. It rocked up and down as she climbed aboard.

She hurried up the steps to the back deck, took shelter under the roof, and gasped for breath. "Made it!"

Still wearing only her bikini, cold and dripping wet, Amy rubbed her shivering arms. Her teeth chattered. What she'd give for a hot shower and a warm robe. No time for that. *At least I'm out of the rain.*

The back door was partially ajar. The boat's interior was dark, save for a few panel lights. Amy opened the glass door all the way, ran inside, and turned on the lights. She froze. Mossy footprints and strips of seaweed littered the floor. Green palm prints had been smeared on the fridge and dining table. One of those walking plant things must have come onboard.

Was it still here? It could be below decks.

She grabbed a fire extinguisher off the wall for a weapon. Keeping her eye on the dark stairway, she went to the helm, picked up the radio handset, and called for help. "Mayday! Mayday!" She twisted the knob looking for a frequency, but all she got was static.

Cursing, she dropped the hand mic. She'd have to call for help later. She had to get back to Jasmine. Then Amy spotted Ted's iPad on the console. If she could get onto the Internet, she could email her parents and let them know she was in need of help. Maybe they could send the local coast guard.

She tapped on the tablet's screen and was immediately disappointed. No Internet signal. Then she realized the line to the satellite dish had been cut. After they'd left Manila, their phones had lost cell service. She was about to put down the iPad when she noticed a folder on the home screen titled AMY AND JASMINE. She opened it. There were two video files inside. She clicked on the first video. It was of her and Jasmine in the bedroom below decks, changing into their bathing suits. Amy felt sick to her stomach. The second video was a wide shot of Jasmine having sex with Dom.

"Those assholes!" Amy growled in anger and slammed the iPad against the console, smashing its screen. Then she threw the tablet out a window into the water.

She squeezed her fists to calm herself down. "Okay, focus, Amy, focus. Get what you need, then get back to Jasmine."

Amy found her beach bag that she'd brought with her. Still wet and shivering, she toweled herself off, then put on a T-shirt and windbreaker. She grabbed Jasmine's windbreaker and stuffed it into the bag.

"Now where's the First-Aid kit?" Amy dug through the galley's drawers and cabinets. She found a flashlight and scuba knife. *These will come in handy*. She strapped the knife's sheath to her bare thigh. Another cabinet delivered a bigger prize: a flare gun with six flares. Her fiancé, Michael, had loved to deep-sea fish off the Florida coast. He had shown her how to use one of these. The orange snub-nosed pistol shot single flares and was used for signaling distress calls at sea. Maybe when the rain stopped, she could shoot a flare over the lagoon. What were the chances a boat would be passing by the island tonight? *Slim*. She hadn't seen one boat since Ted had changed course and cruised through the deserted islands.

We're alone as alone gets.

Although the pistol was designed to shoot in an arc, at close range, it could also be used as a weapon. She loaded a single flare into the breech and stuck it in the pocket of her jacket. A few spares went in her pockets, as well.

In a bottom drawer she found the First-Aid kit. "Bingo!" She loaded all her supplies into her bag. She prayed Jasmine was all right. "Hang tight, sister. I'm coming for you."

Jasmine felt herself growing weaker by the hour. Her numb leg had no feeling when she scratched it. *A phantom leg.* The creature that had bit her must have injected a toxic poison into her bloodstream. Back in college, when she'd volunteered at a hospital, she'd seen swollen snake bites and spider bites that had wilted people's feet and hands. In several cases, the end result was amputation.

I'm going to lose my foot, maybe my whole leg. By the time I reach a hospital, it will be too late to save it.

Holding the machete, Jasmine cried herself to sleep.

She woke in darkness to the feeling of someone pulling her hair. She was seated with her back against the twined sticks that made up the hut's back wall. Another strand of her hair was pulled through a crack and plucked from her head. "Ouch."

She crawled to the middle of the hut, dragging her dead leg. It took a moment to adjust her eyes to the night. Occasional flashes of lightning lit the rain forest outside. Through gaps in the slats, she spotted a silhouette of a skeletal man creeping behind the hut. He had leaves sticking off his shoulders and arms. Bony fingers ran along the wood, making a drawn-out clicking sound like a stick across a fence.

Jasmine gripped the machete. Her heart beat fast, her lips quivered.

It must be the monkey headhunter. I'm in his hut. He's come to collect my head. She imagined her shrunken skull hanging on a vine with all the little monkey skulls.

Still seated, she pivoted as the creeping silhouette made its way around the side wall. The lightning flashes stopped. The forest went dark again.

Amy, please come back, please come back…

Scrapes sounded just outside the hut.

Jasmine dug into her bag and fished out her cell phone. The screen offered faint light. She shined it toward the right side wall. The skeletal man was no longer there. Something thumped just outside the front opening. She panned her light, revealing the spiky dark hair of Dom's head. He crawled along the ground, flat on his belly like he was about to pull a prank on her.

Jasmine felt a flash of hope that he might be alive. "Dom, is that you?"

He raised his head above the floor's level. The skin of his forehead tapered into a glistening, blood-red skull. Jasmine reeled at the green roots that veined across his face, the dark pits of his eyes, the gnashing teeth. His lichen-green tongue clucked like the plants from the jungle. Bony spine humped, Dom's skeleton crawled into the hut, reaching for her.

The rain reduced to a slight drizzle. The clouds parted, and the full moon lit up the lagoon.

Amy climbed down the yacht's stern. She pushed a button that opened the back hatch. Her heart soared with relief as she saw the gray dinghy in its storage compartment. The two-seater raft had two oars and a motor that hung off the back. She pulled it out onto the water, tossed her bag into it, and climbed inside the dingy.

The boat floated strangely, as if she were in a shallow area. All around her kelp drifted across the surface. A large mass of it had piled atop the water and was moving toward her. She pulled out the flare gun and fired. The red flare whizzed over the mass and burst into the water twenty feet away.

Shit. Way to waste a good flare.

Several feelers rose up on the drifting kelp mass as it inched closer. *Move your ass!* She pulled the motor's cord. It didn't start.

The seaweed bunched around the outside of the boat.

Amy pulled the cord again. The motor stuttered then stopped. "Come on!"

The kelp mass was almost upon her. Stalks slid over the edges of the boat. A slimy feeler rubbed across her thigh. Amy swatted it away. She yanked the cord as hard as she could. The motor growled. Its blade cut through the floating kelp.

She guided the motor as the dinghy crossed the dark lagoon. The seaweed retreated under water. Reaching shore, she beached the dinghy.

She ran through the woods to the dark hut. "Jasmine, I'm back."

Her friend didn't respond.

Amy felt acid in the pit of her stomach. She switched on her flashlight. Blood stained the wood floor. Jasmine was gone.

"No…"

The bloody machete was stuck in the middle of the floor. Beside it lay a severed skeletal hand.

Amy grabbed the long blade and spun around, cursing. She spotted drag marks in the sand. It resembled the pattern sea turtles make when they migrate across beaches to lay eggs. This trail, spattered with blood, went around the corner of the hut.

Jasmine, please be alive.

Amy followed the drag marks. They led deeper into the jungle.

Night had cloaked the thick rain forest. Moonlight sifting through the canopy offered some visibility of the trees. The plants that grew near the ground were mostly in shadow.

Somewhere ahead, Jasmine cried out. Amy burst through the bushes. Her flashlight shined on Jasmine's long black hair and head moving along the ground. Her hand clawed at the dirt. "Help!"

A swing of Amy's light beam illuminated a hybrid of a red-muscled skeleton and plants. The thing's back was to her as it ambled through the woods. One of its arms ended in a dripping stump. The other dragged Jasmine by the leg.

"Stop!" Amy yelled.

The corpse halted and half-turned, looking over its shoulder.

Amy's jaw dropped. *Is that…Dom?*

He dropped Jasmine's leg. His foot stepped on her chest as he walked toward Amy.

"Stay away from me." She backed away, all jumbled nerves as her sweaty palms gripped the machete and flashlight.

Dom's mouth opened wide. Nested inside, a dozen green stalks sprung open mouths with needle teeth. The sound of singing cicadas issued from his throat.

Amy tossed the flashlight and wielded the machete.

In the moonlight, the skeletal shadow stepped closer, reaching for Amy. She swung the machete. The blade cracked his shoulder. His elbow struck her in the solar plexus. Knocked her wind out. Amy fell to the ground. Struggled to breathe.

Dom pulled the machete out of his shoulder and tossed it. He rolled Amy over. His sticky body lowered on top of her. She pushed against his chest. Dom's strength overpowered hers. He pinned her to the dirt. A hydra of pods with jaws of needles extended from his throat. Amy screamed, turning her head flat against the ground. She heard a *whack* and Dom's grip slackened. His head titled at an angle on his broken neck. A second *whack* sent the head rolling. Blood spurted from the stump of his neck. The pods trapped inside his ribcage chittered with panic. Amy shoved his writhing carcass off her chest.

Jasmine was up on her knees, holding the machete. She looked in shock from beheading Dom.

Amy rushed into her arms. "Thank God you're alive."

They held each other, crying, grateful to have each other back.

Clicking sounds issued from a few yards away. The bushes rustled on either side of them.

Amy pulled out her flare gun and helped Jasmine to her feet. They stood back to back. Jasmine held the machete. Amy panned the flashlight around the jungle. The beam found a strange-looking bush that seemed to have a face. A monkey-skull necklace dangled across a bony chest. The creature's green tongue clicked fast in its mouth. More clicks responded from Amy's right. Then again from her left. It sounded like insects communicating. There were three of the bush creatures.

Twenty feet away, the leaves rustled. Ted yelled in an altered voice, "You bitches are never leaving this island."

Amy fired a shot in his direction. The flare arced and exploded into a bush. In the flash of red light, she watched Ted's shadow run through the trees. He disappeared into the brush.

The other two rattled off clicks from the surrounding trees.

Amy's shaking hands fumbled to reload her gun. She heard Michael's voice from when he'd taken her deer hunting. *Stay sharp, Amy,* he'd said as she'd trained the rifle's scope on a buck. *Breathe slow and easy...keep your eye on the target.* She sucked in a breath and exhaled as she drove a flare into the pistol's breech. Jasmine, trembling, pressed her back against Amy's.

"I don't want to die," Jasmine whimpered.

"Not without a fight," Amy said. "Stay sharp, sister."

Ten feet away, the bushes shook. Her flashlight beam spotlighted a moving plant, tendrils growing over a skeletal back. The thing was circling them like a predator. She pulled the trigger. A flare shot into the bush. Caught the creature's back on fire. It screeched. Its glowing form dashed a hundred yards through the trees. Then the fiery light vanished. A smaller plant creature ran past and chased after it.

Amy walked Jasmine back to the beach. It was bright now in the moonlight. Amy's gut cramped when she saw the dinghy was no longer tied to the tree. The sound of a motor broke the silence. Ted's silhouette guided the dinghy across the lagoon toward the yacht. Amy's heart sank. Stranded on this hostile island, all hope of surviving seemed lost.

18

The flare pistol at her side, Amy sat in the back corner of the hut with Jasmine resting against her chest. She held her shivering friend. Amy was afraid to turn on the light to look at Jasmine's swollen leg. Last time she did the poison had spread the purple bruise past her knee. Every inch down to her foot had turned black. The skin had wilted. Amy had cleaned up the foot wound as best she could and bandaged it. There was nothing she could do about stopping the poison from spreading. It would probably take a crack team of surgeons to save that leg.

At one point, while Jasmine was passed out, Amy had taken the machete and considered chopping off the rotted limb at mid thigh. Two things made her chicken out: the revulsion she'd feel about cutting off her best friend's leg and the fear of slicing a major artery and killing her. Amy didn't have enough towels and bandages to stop heavy bleeding. She had no fire to cauterize a stump.

Amy kissed Jasmine's head and prayed for her to hold on until help arrived.

Who's going to rescue us? No one knows we're on this island.

You should have tried harder to figure out the radio.

No, if I'd stayed on the boat longer, I wouldn't have gotten back in time. Dom would have taken Jasmine to another part of the island.

Amy couldn't believe what Dom and Ted had become. How the island had fused itself with them. The other two creatures had looked more plant than human. *Is that what's going to happen to Jasmine? Will vines start sprouting from her leg?*

Turn on the light and see. No way. I can't look at it anymore.

Amy was no nurse. She had a weak stomach when it came to seeing people's wounds. The wilted foot had a rancid, fungal smell. After cleaning the pus from the teeth marks, she'd gone outside and vomited. Now she sat in the dark, dreading what lay ahead. She imagined Jasmine's leg splitting open like a pod in the dark. Unseen vines slithering up Jasmine's body and around Amy until they were both cocooned. Then the ivy would feed upon them and turn their carcasses into walking plant habitats.

"Amy?" Jasmine rasped.

"Yes, Jazz."

"I'm sorry for everything."

"Told you, nothing to be sorry about."

"You've always been there for me."

Amy's stomach knotted. "I wish that were true."

"What do you mean?"

"I never should have left you alone at Boyd's. I've always felt guilty for that."

"You shouldn't," Jasmine said. "What he did wasn't your fault."

"But if I hadn't abandoned you…"

"I wouldn't be so fucked up?" Jasmine said.

"I didn't say that."

"No, but you've always thought it. I'm tougher than you think."

"You've been a rock for me," Amy admitted. "After Michael died, you got me through the worst time of my life."

"I know how much you loved him—Michael was a great guy—but you have to move on. Life's too short not to have fun. *Says, the slut,*" Jasmine joked.

Amy laughed. "If we ever get out of this, I'm adding more fun to my bucket list."

"Then you'll jump out of a plane with me?"

"First chance we get."

"I'll have a prosthetic leg."

"Don't say that."

"We don't have to pretend. The leg feels like it's gone already. Definitely going to be an amputee." Then she added, "If I make it."

Amy didn't respond. She couldn't deal with talking about that right now.

Jasmine sniffled. "I was thinking about the jewelry shop we planned to open."

"Planned? That's still happening," Amy said. "Now, that you and I are together again, we're going to lease a building in Ojai and open up shop. We'll design a fancy logo and hang a big sign over the front door," Amy said.

"Sounds nice," Jasmine said.

"In the evenings, we'll sit out on a patio and drink wine with other artists in town."

"Mm-hmm."

"Just hold on to our dream, sister. It's gonna happen."

"I love you, Amers."

"Love you too, Jazz." Amy squeezed her tight against her chest. No snuggling with pillow man tonight. *Just me and my bestie.*

19

In the lagoon, floating mounds of kelp formed a protective barrier around the yacht. Ted sat on the back deck, facing the beach. The drizzling rain fed the green horticulture that covered his body, renewing his strength. He felt ivy roots moving through his brain. He smiled like a man blissed out on opium. He was taken back to his happiest days, a sated boy lying in his mother's arms. He saw Mother's face. Not the mean-drunk one, the affectionate one, when she was young and beautiful and smiled as she caressed him tenderly and sang whispery songs into his ear. His time with her was too short, though, as Mother dissolved away, leaving him in a lonely blackness. Then Amy appeared, half-naked, the parts he so wanted to gaze upon hidden in the shadows, her blonde hair hanging over her breasts. Ted's body filled with desire, unfulfilled lust, and a burning want to make her his. He felt propelled to go back to the beach, take her while she slept. The ivy woven around his bones tightened, restrained him from moving from his spot. Ted growled, fought against the plants.

From the island's center, the elders whispered in his mind.

The mental image of Amy backed away into the darkness.

At peace again, he watched the moonlit beach and jungle. His consciousness connected to every bush, every tree, every fungus, and to the others who had become like him. The guardians. They were going into a stasis, lying inside dank, hollow places with ivy closing over them. One of them was wounded with burns. Ted felt its pain. Like the others, he fell into a trance. His opium-smile returned as the elders whispered what they wanted him to do.

20

Morning light leaked through the slats of the walls. Amy opened her eyes. She didn't remember falling asleep. She whispered, "Hey, girl, you awake?"

Jasmine felt heavy in her arms. Her body heat had cooled. Amy checked her friend's neck for a pulse. Couldn't find one. Jasmine's head lolled on her shoulder. Her mouth hung open.

"No..." Amy cried. "Stay with me." She shook her. "Jasmine! Jasmine, wake up!"

She lay her friend on her back and desperately tried performing CPR, breathing into Jasmine's mouth. "Breathe! Breathe!" Amy shouted over and over as her hands pumped thirty chest compressions. Then she breathed into her mouth again and repeated the compressions for several minutes.

Jasmine remained still and limp. Her eyes were half open. Blank. Dead eyes.

Amy put a hand over her own mouth. Tears streamed down her cheeks. She sobbed and sobbed, rocking her friend's body in her arms.

Sometime later, after she had cried out all her tears and her eyes were raw, Amy whispered a prayer. She draped a towel over Jasmine's body, caressed her cold cheek, then covered her face.

Amy was too numb to know what to do next. She stepped out of the hut and walked in a half daze through the trees toward the beach.

The quiet of the morning was interrupted by the growl of a motor. The yacht cruised toward the mouth of the lagoon. A realization hit Amy with a jolt. *Ted's leaving me behind!* Her only means of escape disappeared into the narrow channel between the mangroves.

Feelings of terror and abandonment coursed through her, rising up her body like a geyser. She released an animal cry and pounded her fist against a palm tree. An approaching sound broke her out of her tantrum. She hid behind the tree and listened. A moment later, the white yacht whirred back into the lagoon.

Ted's coming back to get me.

The boat didn't slow down. Instead, the motor growled as the yacht picked up speed. The bow hopped across the water, headed straight toward the beach. With an ear-splitting boom, it ran aground in the shallow water and hop-skipped halfway up the beach. The bow crashed into the trees. The stern remained in the water, but the propeller spun to a halt in the mud. Then the engine died.

Amy's only other escape, the dinghy, had floated far out into the lagoon overnight, and seaweed now covered it.

21

With no way off the island and her best friend dead, Amy considered cutting her wrists and lying down next to Jasmine. Soul sisters born together, it seemed somehow poetic they should die together. But Amy had too much survival instinct to end her own life. When Michael had died before their wedding, Amy had wanted to die with him, but couldn't bring herself to leave Jasmine behind. And during the dark years that she and Jasmine were separated, when suicide sounded like such an easy way out, Amy couldn't follow through on it. All along she had thought her fear of abandoning Jasmine was the drive that kept Amy going. But now that her friend was gone, Amy was discovering a force inside her that propelled her to keep living. She also felt a fire burning in her chest, a boiling in her blood, for revenge against Ted, the bush creatures, and this island that had taken away the one person Amy had loved most.

Clutching the machete and gripping the flare gun, scuba knife strapped to her bare thigh, she walked down the beach toward the yacht. It lay silent as a dead beached whale, with a gentle tide lapping against the back of its hull. Windows that curved the length of the cabin were covered in sand. There was no sign of Ted. The impact of the crash could have killed him.

Amy wasn't taking any chances.

He could still be inside, waiting for me. She hadn't seen him get off the boat. Then again, she'd taken her eyes off it while she formulated her next plan. First priority was to chop up Ted into a dozen gory pieces. Second: see if the radio still worked and call for help. Third: search the galley for food. A ravenous hunger ached in her belly, partly for food, partly for vengeance. She aimed to satiate her appetite for both.

Keeping a wary eye on the jungle to her left, she eased up to the boat. Rounding the stern, she waded through shin-deep water while watching the lagoon. The kelp had retreated underwater. The shallow area around her feet was crystal clear. Nothing but sand, shells, and some fish bones. She imagined the killer kelp ate any sea animals that made their way into the lagoon.

Amy quietly climbed up the rear steps onto the deck. The back window and thick glass door had spiderwebs of cracks.

She pulled open the door.

Sand covered the windows, making the interior of the cabin gloomy. The galley and dining area were empty. She rounded the cockpit, expecting to find Ted's dead body crumpled near the windshield. No such luck. The situation looked grimmer when she saw the state of the control panel. All the computer screens were off and cracked. Worst of all, Ted had torn out the radio and cut the wires and mic cord.

Hot tears burned behind Amy's eyes. She didn't cry. Anger replaced her sadness as she squeezed the machete.

Where are you, motherfucker?

Past the cockpit, stairs led down to the below decks area. It was dark down there. Ted could be hiding in one of the two cabins, the bunk area, or the bathroom.

No way I'm going down there.

She backed away from the stairs. A basket of fruit and snacks had dumped into the sink and onto the floor. She peeled a banana and devoured it as she watched the stairs. She was so famished, she ripped open a granola bar with her teeth and wolfed it down. She had to pace herself. She might have to make this food last.

A *whirring* sound came from somewhere outside.

She poked her head out the back door. A small yellow plane was flying in the distance, headed this way. Her heart soared. She ran onto the back deck, held up her flare gun, and waited for the right moment.

"Come closer, come closer."

The prop plane kept getting bigger as it approached. "Yes, yes!"

Amy was about to fire when the sound of thumping came from behind her. She turned in time to see Ted leap off the cabin's roof. He knocked her onto her back. The impact of her head banging the floor left her dazed. The pistol and machete slid out of her hands.

Ted pinned her to the deck. His fleshless body was a green ruin. His ears, nose, and lips were gone. The lichen feeding on him had left only an island of skin on the left side of his face, along with his one good eye. He stared at her just like Boyd had. A sexual predator ogling his prey.

His mossy hand gripped her jaw. His hand glided over her breast, squeezed hard. "We'll live forever on this island, and you will do whatever I please."

She could feel his pelvis was missing some key anatomy. She glanced down at his hollow crotch. "Looks like the plants have eaten your manhood off."

"I still got my tongue." The spore-covered thing in his mouth clicked fast.

She turned her head in disgust. The flare gun lay under the deck's table, out of reach.

"No need to worry about my manhood," he breathed. "Once I take you to the sanctuary and deliver you to the island, we'll mate in a whole new way."

"Where's the sanctuary?" she asked to distract him. Her free hand pressed against her thigh and gripped the scuba knife. She slowly slid it out of its sheath.

"Center of the island. It's where the elders live. They want you as much as I do. Now, you can go willingly, or I can drag you there. Take your pick."

"I'll pick the third option."

"What's that?"

She stabbed the knife into his ribs fast several times. Black blood spilled out. He gripped his side, leaped off of her, and bellowed.

She rolled over and crawled toward the gun. He gripped her ankle and pulled her back. She turned and sliced the blade across his bony chest. Green ooze spattered the deck and walls. He fell back against the stern rail. He looked down at the damage her blade had done and laughed. "You're a feisty one. Guess it's gonna take some pain to teach you to obey." He started toward her.

Amy reached under the table, pulled the flare gun out, and pulled the trigger at close range. The flare burst into the center of his chest and sparkled inside his ribcage. With a shocked expression, he stumbled back and fell overboard into the lagoon.

Amy grabbed the machete and ran to the rail.

Down below, Ted floated on his back with a small fire burning inside his chest. The lapping waves quickly extinguished it. The tide pulled him toward the middle of the lagoon. The seaweed wrapped around him like tentacles and pulled him underwater.

Amy watched for a long time. He didn't resurface. When she looked up at the sky, her rescue plane was a yellow dot flying far off into the distance.

PART THREE

Survival

22

Three days passed. Amy's world was reduced to a sliver of beach shaped like a sickle that wrapped around the lagoon. She stayed away from the jungle and water. At least she had the wrecked boat for shelter. She'd made herself at home inside, her five-star luxury beach shack. If she had to be marooned on an island, it might as well be first class. She'd cleaned sand off all the windows to let sunlight in. During the daylight hours, she felt safer because she could see if anyone was trying to sneak up on her from the jungle. Nights were the hardest. The jungle made all kinds of chittering-cracking-rustling sounds. She locked herself inside the master stateroom and slept on its queen bed. She had terrible nightmares. In one vivid dream, hundreds of vines pulled her boat deep into the jungle. Tree limbs broke through her windows. The jungle invaded her bedroom. Vines tied her to the bed, then tore off her T-shirt. Naked, she fought against her restraints as leafy fingers crawled over her skin. The door burst open and Dom's and Ted's plant-covered corpses ambled into the room. They groped her as they climbed onto the bed. Amy woke up screaming. At first light, she ran upstairs to make sure the boat was still on the beach.

The next night she dreamt of Jasmine, eleven-years-old, her small body crouched and shivering in the corner of the cabin, wrapped in her beach towel. She was sobbing, just like she had the night the police walked her out of Boyd Kuczek's house. Jasmine repeated the first angry words she'd said to Amy after the incident. *"How could you leave me with him?"*

Still in bed, watching poor little Jasmine cry, Amy felt someone moving under the covers behind her. A man with a hairy body hugged her. Rough hands pawed her breasts. Boyd pressed his bearded cheek against hers. "You should have stayed and played Natives with us."

Amy threw back the covers, leaped off the bed, and backed away.

In the gloom, Boyd's shadow sat up on the bed. He pulled a tribal mask of a demon over his face.

Grabbing her machete, she shielded young Jasmine in the corner. "I won't let you hurt us!"

Jasmine whispered in Amy's ear, "You're too late."

When Amy woke up, she was sitting in the corner of her bedroom, gripping the machete. The ghosts of Boyd and Jasmine had vanished with the night.

By the third morning, it took all of Amy's faith to keep her spirits up. She maintained hope that her being stranded was only temporary, that a boat would arrive or a pontoon plane would fly overhead and see her flare. *I just need to survive a couple more days, a week at most.*

She imagined a huge task force of Philippine Coast Guard combing through the islands on boats. A squadron of prop planes flying over each island in search of the missing Americans. Their story was probably international news by now. She pictured her worried parents watching CNN, a montage of photos of Amy and Jasmine above the latest headlines. *Don't give up on me yet,* she wanted to tell Mom and Dad. *They're going to find me.*

Trying to hang onto the person she once was, Amy followed a strict routine, just like she'd done at home. In the mornings, she practiced yoga, meditated, bathed—in this case, wiping herself down with a wet rag to preserve what little water she had on the boat. She ate breakfast—a ration of fruit, potato chips, and granola bars—then went about her day. Mostly she sat on the aft deck with the flare gun, watching the sky for planes and the lagoon's mangrove channel for boats.

This morning, Amy didn't want to go to the hut. But after her latest nightmare, she felt guilt-ridden for abandoning Jasmine, even though she was over three days dead. Amy found her friend's corpse right where she'd left it. Jasmine's body had bloated to the point the beach towel no longer covered all of it. Amy entered the hut, one hand covering her mouth and nose. Thin green tendrils had grown through cracks in the floorboards and attached themselves to the corpse's flesh. More vines had come through the gaps in the rear stick wall and wrapped around Jasmine's head.

Amy chopped at the vines with her machete. The severed green limbs released a painful shriek and slithered back out of the hut. The towel covering Jasmine moved, as if a bed of snakes squirmed beneath it. Amy reached for the towel, terrified of what she might find underneath. By now, every plant species on the island could have taken refuge in her decomposing body. An overpowering stench made Amy gag. As she pulled the towel partly away, Jasmine's head rolled to one side. A beard of moving lichen covered her lower jaw. Green tendrils poked out of a hole in her gray swollen cheek.

Amy lost her nerve and hurried back outside. She paced, crying over what the jungle had done to her friend. *I should go back in there and chop her up. Obliterate every damned plant nesting inside her.*

Amy couldn't bring herself to do it, though. Jasmine's death was still too fresh. The pain of losing her a constant ache in Amy's heart.

It was hard to believe that just days ago they had been checking into their hotel and talking about the fun week they would spend in tropical paradise. They were supposed to relax for a week by the hotel's pool. Hit the spa a few times. Drink tropical drinks at the bar. *Now my best friend is dead and I have to destroy her body?* Amy shook her head at the dreadful thought. She backed away from the hut. *I can't, I just can't.*

Something in a clearing behind the hut caught her eye. Curious, she rounded the back corner and discovered a grave with a wooden cross. The name GWYN had been carved into the horizontal plank. Who was Gwyn? Another victim to this evil island?

Seeing the grave made her wonder if she should bury Jasmine. *No,* Amy decided. When she got rescued—and it was going to happen any day now, damn it—she wanted to take her friend's body with her, even if it was nothing more than a skeleton that had been picked clean by scavenger plants. Jasmine deserved a proper burial in California. Her parents would want that.

God, Jasmine's mom and dad... How am I going to explain to them what happened?

Jasmine's parents were strict but kind to people they liked, especially to Amy. When they were kids, Amy had slept over at Jasmine's house often. Her mother cooked the best spicy curry dinners and took them roller skating or to the park. Her father was usually busy writing sermons that he'd give at church on Sundays, so they mostly saw him at dinner.

On other nights, the girls had sleepovers at Amy's house and swam or watched movies well past bedtime. Amy's parents would be devastated, too, at the loss. Jasmine had been like a second daughter to them. Amy's mom and dad had felt heartbroken after discovering their friend, Boyd, had molested their daughter and her friend during one of their parties. The sleepovers at Amy's had ended after that, due to a rift between their parents. But as the girls became teenagers and later college roommates, they had visited each other's parents many times, celebrating birthdays and Thanksgivings, playing Canasta, Mahjong, and Scrabble.

Amy put those memories out of her mind. Thoughts about home only threw her into an emotional tailspin.

I need to stay strong. Focus on survival. Don't want to end up six feet under like Gwyn, or worse, like the others.

She sensed someone watching her from the jungle. The bush creatures? She hadn't seen them since the night she burned the tall one. Amy felt vulnerable this close to the wall of trees and brush. She walked back down to the beach. When she reached the yacht, there was a message drawn in the wet sand: SURRENDER.

She looked into the jungle to see if anyone was watching her. Then she erased the message. With her knife, she carved her own message: NEVER.

23

On the fifth day, the boat's battery died. She no longer had light or use of appliances. She didn't need the fridge anymore. It was empty. She had maybe enough drinkable water to last a week if she rationed carefully. With chapped lips and a dry throat, it was hard not to drink more than a sip at a time. She was currently rationing her last bag of chips and half a granola bar—two chips and two pinches a day. Hunger was her constant companion.

As Amy sat on the back deck watching for planes, she kept eyeing the green coconuts in the palm trees that grew beyond the mangroves. Her mouth watered just thinking about breaking into a coconut and drinking its milk.

To get the fruit, she'd have to hike through the mangrove forest. Did mangroves attack like the other flesh-eating plants? She was scared to go in there.

I have to figure out how to survive a little longer. Need to learn how to make a fire too, so I can have light at night. She had a lighter and some spare cans of fuel that might come in handy for starting campfires, but she needed to preserve them. She was afraid to think about what the boat would be like tonight once night fell.

Amy couldn't sleep. She lay in the pitch darkness of her bedroom. Footsteps thumped on the upper deck. Someone was in the galley!

Her heart jumped. She became short of breath. She turned on her flashlight. All her weapons lay next to the bed, within reach. The knife didn't seem to faze the hybrids. The machete would most likely take several chops to bring down an intruder. She chose the flare gun. *Two flares left. Don't waste them.*

Gripping the pistol in her sweaty palms, she watched the ceiling.

Whoever was up there was banging things around. Metal clanged, like a pot falling into the sink. *Shit, I forgot to secure my food.* Hearing a noise outside, she had run downstairs to her room and left her food on the counter. If the intruder destroyed her small food supply, Amy feared she would starve to death in a matter of days. If she survived tonight.

Stay positive, she told herself.

It could be someone who's just arrived on the island. A coast guard member who has a boat to take me away from here. The thought of being rescued lifted her spirits briefly. Then her mind filled with doubt. *If the coast guard had arrived, wouldn't there be more people walking around, voices? I never heard a boat's engine, or even the tide lapping against the yacht's stern from the boat's approach.*

Maybe they paddled a small dinghy to shore, although that seemed less likely than arriving by motorboat.

Amy felt torn. She wanted to go upstairs, see who was on her boat. She wanted to switch off her light and hide in the darkness until whoever it was went away. Her mind argued back and forth. *Open that door and the hybrids will get me. This could be my one chance to be rescued.*

She got up and started toward the door. She almost opened it when she heard a familiar *click-click-clicking*, like the rubbing of insect wings, a sound just like the bush creature's tongue had made.

The footsteps above clomped directly over her room toward the bow. Whatever it was had a shambling, uneven gait with branch-like scrapes.

Amy backed a few feet from the door, tightening her grip on the flare gun. She watched the ceiling and listened as the footsteps descended the stairs. *Clomp…clomp…clomp…*

The footsteps approached the bedroom door. Nails dragged down the wood.

Amy…, Jasmine's ghostly voice spoke inside Amy's head. *Let me in.*

Amy trembled as she aimed her pistol.

Nails continued to scratch the door. *Open up, Amy.*

"Stay away from me!"

Surrender with me. We'll be together again.

"Go away," Amy pleaded. "I don't want to hurt you…"

Boyd's here with me.

A man's husky breath reverberated in Amy's head. *Come out and play with us.*

"It's not them," Amy whispered. "It's just the island fucking with my mind."

A rustling sound came from beyond the door. At the bottom, ropy purple feelers slinked through the crack. A dozen of them slid up the door. The feelers wrapped around the knob and undid the latch. The door creaked as it slowly swung open. In the blackness beyond the threshold stood Jasmine's writhing shadow. The hybrid of her and the jungle was an abomination of bones and plants. It released a high-pitched clicking like a swarm of locusts.

Amy's flashlight beam traced up skeletal green legs to a ribcage overgrown with vines that undulated like the arms of an octopus. Her long black hair draped over bony, lichen-covered shoulders. Where Jasmine's face had once been there was now a large hole in her skull, like a broken porcelain doll. A nest of orchids wriggled within the cavity. The corpse of her best friend raised its arms. Stalks moved out of her head. On their tips, flowers opened. Mouths circled with sharp teeth opened deeper to expose slimy pink throats with pistil tongues.

The plant-thing shrieked and rushed through the door. Ivy wrapped around Amy's waist and legs. She fought to break free, but its grip was too tight. As the hybrid pulled her toward a head of hungry orchids, Amy fired the gun point blank. A flare shot straight into the hole of Jasmine's skull, burst the entire head into flame, and spiraled down into her ribcage.

The hybrid screeched. Its appendages slapped the walls and ceiling. Lighting up like a torch, it released Amy and dashed out of the room and up the stairs.

Driven by madness, Amy grabbed the machete and chased after it. The hybrid ran all the way to the beach before collapsing in the sand. The flowers unleashed a thousand cries of pain.

Amy stood over the creature, raised the machete, and chopped off its head. The skull with scorched black hair rolled down to the water's edge. All the plants and flowers along its body wilted and burned to cinders. When her friend's deformed skeleton was nothing more than blackened bones, Amy fell to her knees and cried.

24

A part of Amy died after cremating her friend's undead corpse. As the tide pushed Jasmine's burnt skull along the shore, Amy felt the last of her humanity slipping away. She vacillated between crying and laughing hysterically to periods of silent brooding.

The game had changed. No longer did she fantasize about being rescued or ever seeing home again. The Amy who had been a jewelry designer, loving friend, and daughter was dead. She had been reduced to a primal need to survive. The island had shown that it intended to use everything in its power to defeat her. It was kill or be killed.

I won't let this fucking island take me without a fight.

When the tears were gone, she worked around the boat with stubborn determination. She skipped her yoga routine. Ate the last morsels of her food supply. She buried Jasmine's ashes along with her skull and broken bones in the graveyard behind the monkey hut, next to the cross that read *GWYN*. Amy carved Jasmine's name on a second cross. As she gave a eulogy, praying for God to watch over her soul sister, something moved in the bushes twenty yards away.

Amy made out the face of a plant creature that might have once been a little girl. Long, dirty strands of brown hair hung from its skull and down its shoulders. White mushrooms filled the eye sockets. Its mouth opened, revealing green needle teeth that dripped saliva that was certainly filled with venom. Jasmine had mentioned a child-sized creature that bit her foot and injected her with a stinging poison. Now, the creature croaked and shook the bushes like an angry ape defending its territory.

Amy raised her machete and gun, let out a warrior cry, and charged toward the bush.

The child hybrid squawked and retreated into the jungle.

When Amy got back to the boat, she found another message drawn in the sand: COME INTO JUNGLE. Had the child written it or its elder?

Amy scrawled her own message in the sand: COME TO THE BEACH.

If she had to fight the hybrids, she'd rather it be on her turf.

25

On the seventh day, a storm battered the island. Rain thumped against the boat's roof and plinked in catch-water pans out on the deck. She ran across the deck, emptying the pans into the boat's reservoir and setting them out again. Then she drank until her thirst was quenched, but even the fresh supply of drinking water wasn't enough to lift Amy's dark mood. She sat wet and shivering inside the upper deck cabin with a blanket wrapped around her. The world outside her windows was wet and gray. The poor visibility would keep planes from spotting the wrecked boat. And the storm would keep Amy from hearing the plane's engines. Another day wasted. She needed to go out and search for food.

She was so hungry now her guts cramped. It felt like her body was caving in on itself. She had bad diarrhea and made several trips to the toilet. She barely recognized herself in the bathroom mirror. Her face had turned gaunt. Her ribs were visible through her skin. *I'm a walking skeleton.*

She'd once read the human body could last three weeks without food. Gandhi had starved himself twenty-one days and survived. She smiled briefly, thinking she was now following the path of one of her heroes. *Maybe I'll become enlightened and my plight will inspire the world.*

Except the world will never know what happened to me. My story will be nothing more than a blip on the news—"Missing American travelers in the Philippines never found. The coast guard is calling off the search." People would write them off and move on to other, more pressing news. Her parents, who had never been driven enough to accomplish long-term goals, would give up and deal with their loss the way they always did, getting stoned. Like so many times during her years that followed her night with Boyd Kuczek, Amy felt abandoned.

As the rain fell and made constant rings on the lagoon, she fantasized about food, recalling the seafood dinner she'd enjoyed with Jasmine, Dom, and Ted back in Manila that first night—lobster, prawns, and fish with garlic-butter mashed potatoes and steamed vegetables, bottles of red wine, followed by large slices of chocolate fudge cake with ice cream. Little had they known it would be their last feast.

They're all dead, and it's just me now. Just me.

Amy's stomach gurgled.

I have to find food.

Her craving for coconuts finally beat out her fear of venturing too far from the yacht. She armed herself with her three amigos: Pistol, Machete, and Knife. She carried an empty beach bag over her shoulder.

She looked down at the beach to check this morning's sand message: COME INTO JUNGLE.

Carving the sand with her knife, Amy politely responded: FUCK OFF!

Taking a deep breath, she waded through the knee-deep water into the dense forest of mangroves. The branches moved in the breeze but didn't attack. Thankfully, there was no killer kelp in the clear shallow water. Several channels cut through the groves. Amy sloshed across one channel to the next until she found a dry, sandy area with scattered coconut trees. Brown and green coconuts littered the ground. The brown husks had split open and dried out. Amy eagerly chopped a green coconut open and drank every last drop of its sweet juice in one gulp. Then she scraped out the pulp and ate it. She had never gotten so much pleasure from eating. She was thrilled to discover an abundant source of food. This part of the island, which was mostly mangroves and spaced-apart coconut trees, seemed safe from the carnivorous plants and vines that inhabited the jungle.

Satiated and feeling strong again, Amy loaded her beach bag with coconuts. As she crossed back through the mangroves, something white caught her eye. Down one of the narrow channels, covered in tree limbs, was a shipwrecked boat listing to one side. She approached it cautiously. The boat was smaller than her yacht. This one looked to be about a thirty-footer. A deep-sea fishing boat like the one Michael used to take her out on. Weather and age had taken its toll. The rotted hull had a few holes in it.

There could be food on board! A bag of chips or a Snickers bar. Oh, what she'd give for chocolate right now. Even the possibility of it lifted her spirits higher than they'd been in a long while.

The interior smelled of mold and mildew. She rummaged through the cupboards and drawers. All she found were empty sardine and Vienna sausage tins and an empty jar of Vegemite. Her spirits plummeted. Whoever had been shipwrecked on this island had eaten every last morsel.

She sat at the dining table and rested her forehead on her hand. She didn't even try to be strong-willed to stop the tears, just let them fall and her body rock with the sobs. When the sadness passed, she sniffled and opened her eyes. A faded photo of a family was tucked in the window. In the picture a middle-age man wearing a skipper hat stood next to an attractive woman with short brown hair, and a pretty freckle-faced girl, about nine, who resembled her mother. They were posing on a dock with this boat behind them. Handwriting on the backside read: *Skipper Jim, Gwyn, and Ellie Walker, Darwin Harbour, summer voyage 2015.*

Amy remembered the grave by the hut.

She found a skipper's log book dated the same year as the photo. The Australian family, seeking to "get out of the rat race" for their holiday, had voyaged to the Philippines and made the mistake of visiting the lagoon of this island.

Day seven: Found ourselves a piece of hidden paradise in the Philippines, 12.3795° N, 124.6840° E. The secluded island appears uninhabited. Ellie and I swam while Gwyn soaked up some rays on the beach. Later, I tried to do some fishing, but nothing in the lagoon was biting. All I reeled in was seaweed. Spending the night on the boat. Tomorrow after brekkie, we're going to explore the island. Gwyn and Ellie want to pick some exotic flowers. Ellie hopes we'll see some monkeys. There must be some on the island. Near the beach we found a hut decorated with monkey skulls. Someone must have lived on this island long ago.

Day eight: Ellie's having a rough go of it. She says she was sniffing some orchids and they sprayed sap into her nose. Gave her face a strawberry rash. Poor girl's been sneezing in fits. Still waiting on Gwyn to get back from the jungle. On the other side of a stream, she spotted papaya trees and went to pick some fruit for dessert. Wish she would hurry back. Ellie and I are ready to eat these hotdogs we've been roasting over a campfire.

Day nine: Beyond worried. Gwyn never came back last night. I pray she didn't get lost in the jungle. Ellie's gotten sicker. Rash has spread from her face to her chest. Need to get her to a doctor. I have to find Gwyn.

Day eleven: Ellie died in my arms yesterday. I'm so devastated I can barely do anything but cry. I can't believe my baby girl is gone. I had to store Ellie's body in the forward fish box. The smell had gotten so bad. Gwyn is still missing.

Day twelve: Last night I heard bumping noises on the deck. I went outside to investigate and found green slimy hand prints and footprints. The fish box was empty. Someone took Ellie's body.

Day fifteen: Gwyn and Ellie came back, but they've changed. Mutated. They look dead, but somehow alive. Plants are growing on them. My wife and daughter are not alone. A plant-covered thing that walks erect on two legs has been on the island all along, watching us. It might have once been a man, someone who got stranded here like us, but it's far from human now.

Day sixteen: Something's terribly wrong with this bloody island. It won't let me leave. The kelp got into the motor. My boat won't start. Gwyn, Ellie, and the bush man have been stalking me. Gwyn, who speaks in a strange voice, referred to him as "the guardian" and asked me to join them in the jungle. I barely recognize my wife and daughter. When I approached them, they tried to kill me.

Day thirty-one: I've had little motivation to write. Stay drunk most days. I killed the thing my wife had become. It wasn't her, I keep telling myself. The island killed my dear Gwyn over two weeks ago. Now, it's just me playing cat and mouse with the guardian and my daughter. I got too close to Ellie and she bit my hand. Her teeth are damned toxic. I used a snake-bite kit to get the venom out, but still feel sick. Staring hard at the barrel of my pistol.

The log rambled on for several more pages as Skipper Jim reflected on the life he, Gwyn, and Ellie had left behind in Sydney and his regrets bringing his family to this island. Amy turned to the final recorded days.

Day thirty-two: At last, I killed the old guardian. I shot it several times and cut off its head. It wore a monkey-skull necklace which I kept to show the island I've defeated it. The bite on my hand keeps getting infected. Plants have been sprouting around the wound. I feel things squirming in my guts.

Day thirty-three: I've given up hope of rescue. The island has gotten into my body and inside my head. The thing that was once my sweet little Ellie keeps calling me to surrender to the island, to become its guardian with her. I have no more strength to resist. This is my last entry. Today, I'm abandoning my boat and going into the jungle to join my daughter.

Amy closed the book with a heavy feeling in her heart. The excitement she had felt finding the coconuts was now replaced with a deep sense of sadness for the Australian family and dread for her own life. At least two guardians remained.

26

She'd lost track of time reading the diary and foraging through the fishing boat. In a cupboard, she found a flask with an engraved anchor and the inscription *Skipper Jim Walker, great husband and father* on the front. On the back: *Love always, Gwyn and Ellie.* The silver container was half-full with some strong-smelling whiskey.

Raising the flask to the boat's ceiling, she said, "Here's to you and your family, Skipper Jim." A couple gulps made her cough, then came the burn in her chest. She drank until she got a buzz. Already tired from the hike, she dozed off while seated at the family's dining table. She woke up later a little dizzy.

She laughed. "I have to stay off the booze."

When she climbed out, it was dusk. The setting sun winked through the trees to the west. Deep shadows filled the mangroves. The lagoon beyond was getting even darker.

"Oh, shit." *I have to get back to the boat before nightfall.*

Lugging her bag of coconuts, she weaved between the trees. She sloshed through the knee-deep water as fast as she could and entered a graveyard of shipwrecked boats. A dozen more fishing boats and skiffs had been overtaken by the mangroves. Water completely filled a small rusted metal motorboat. One rotting wooden vessel covered in mushrooms looked as if it had been here for decades. There was no time to explore them. The last vestiges of daylight faded fast as she crossed between the broken boats. When the sun sank below the horizon, her heart filled with panic. The only safe place after dark was locking herself in her bedroom.

Click-click-clicking sounded to her left.

The hairs stood on her neck.

She set down her bag, gripped her machete, and switched on her flashlight. The mangroves' thick bushy treetops and exposed roots offered plenty of hiding places. Her beam caught leafy movement through the groves. A tall, scarecrow-thin body, overgrown with vines and moss, crept toward her. She spotlighted a man's skeletal face. Part of his head and shoulder were badly charred from the flare she'd hit him with a few nights ago. One gnarled arm hung useless. He moved slowly, hunched like a decrepit old man. In addition to ivy, his face, chest, and back were covered in bark mushrooms. He had no eyes, but he behaved as if he saw her.

"Is that you, Skipper Jim Walker?" Amy asked.

He stopped, tilted his head as if he recognized the name. Despite being more plant than human, there was still a hint of humanity in his mannerisms. Unlike Dom and Jasmine, whose corpses had been reanimated by the plants, this thing that had once been the skipper was different. More self-aware. Cautious even, as if it recognized Amy as a threat. Was Skipper Jim's consciousness still a part of the hybrid? Ted's hybrid had been aware too and could even speak. Amy wondered if fusing with the island while still alive kept one's soul intact. If Skipper Jim had any awareness of the man he once was, then perhaps he had memories.

She dug into her bag and pulled out the photo of the Walkers standing on the dock. She held the photo in the light. He seemed to stare at it curiously.

"I know about what happened to you and your family." Amy eased toward him, clutching the machete. "It's awful what this island did to Gwyn and Ellie."

He shuddered at the mention of their names.

"I'm sorry the island killed your wife and daughter. I lost someone I loved too. She died in my arms just like Ellie died in yours."

He clucked his tongue softly, a mournful sound.

"It's not your fault what this island did to you," she said. "Over five years is a long time to be marooned on this purgatory. I bet you've suffered enough. I can end your misery."

Amy stepped within ten feet. Holding up the machete, she readied herself for the guardian's next move. He looked too damaged to put up much of a fight. He bent over even more, head turned and looking up at her like a dog submitting to its master. Then he began clicking his tongue fast. Suddenly, water splashed and branches began cracking off to Amy's right. A child-sized hybrid burst from the darkness. Amy whirled around. Her light found an impossibly wide mouth with green needle teeth. Her arm reflexively swung the machete. The blade lopped off the small creature's head. Its body ran past Amy and collapsed in the shallow water.

The hybrid that had been the little girl's father wailed. He fell to his knees and cradled the small headless corpse in his arms. He rocked her, his whole body shaking as if sobbing.

Amy's adrenaline was racing from the attack. Guilt struck her chest, as she realized she'd just killed Ellie. It pained her heart to watch a father mourn over the death of his child. No, it was no longer the sweet girl Skipper Jim had described in his journal. Nor was he innocent. He had attempted to distract Amy, pretending to be weak while his fellow hunter moved in for the kill. The Ellie-hybrid's venomous teeth had almost bitten Amy, just like the girl had bitten and poisoned Jasmine. Rage burned through Amy. Despite their traces of humanity, these two were guardians of the island and would have killed her.

"It's over, Skipper Jim. It's time to join your wife and daughter." Amy raised the machete over her shoulder. Looking up at her, Skipper Jim tilted his head, exposing his neck. He remained still as the executioner's blade came down.

27

Amy felt at peace as she carried the heavy beach bag through the mangroves. Along with several coconuts, inside her bag was the tall guardian's severed head. She'd even kept his monkey-skull necklace and flask. The spoils of a war that was finally over. *And I won. I'm the lone survivor.* She would sleep peacefully tonight. Her queen bed was calling her.

As she neared the edge of the mangroves, rippling light brightened the lagoon. She heard crackling fire. Had someone else come to the island? She waded faster down a channel and stepped into the shallow area of the lagoon. Gasping, she dropped her bag and placed a hand over her mouth. At the beach, her yacht was on fire.

"No!" she cried.

She rushed to the beach. Flames filled the interior cabin. They spread across the bow and stern. Everything she'd left onboard was in that inferno—her spare clothes, blankets, towels. Her last bottles of drinking water. She smelled gasoline and saw the two gas cans on the beach. In the sand beside them was a carved message: YOU'RE ALL MINE, BITCH.

Amy unleashed a guttural, primal scream. She clutched her pistol and machete and yelled at the jungle. "Come out and fight!"

"Come into the jungle!" Ted called back.

She shot a flare in the direction of his voice. It turned a tree into a red sparkler. She glimpsed a hideous shadow as a Ted-plant hybrid dashed through the trees. "Better not fall asleep!" he called before he disappeared into the dark jungle.

All across the island, the plants made night-cricket clicks and singing cicada songs. Even the lagoon filled with sounds as the kelp raised feelers that splashed the water.

Amy stood on the beach, shaking with anger and fear.

How am I gonna survive the night?

She sat in the sand with the burning boat to her back. It kept her warm. She fought hard not to fall asleep. So tired. All she wanted to do was lie down in the sand and close her eyes. *No, I can't fall asleep. Stay awake.* She feared if she allowed her eyelids to close, Ted would come and take her. She was so exhausted she probably wouldn't realize what was happening until he'd dragged her deep into the forest.

She felt him watching. He stayed hidden within the darkness, a patient predator.

28

Sleep betrayed her. In strange dreams, she received visions that played behind her eyes like a continuous time-lapse movie. The island rock rising out of the water, turning green with vegetation, evolving into its own exotic plant kingdom, protecting itself against intruders. Over centuries, countless wooden ships, schooners, and modern boats had mistakenly visited the island. Explorers fell victim to its hunger. Some men and women became food, their bones offerings to the elders. Others became guardians, replacing the weaker predecessors that had rotted and died off. Amy witnessed the fifteen Filipino passengers of the white double-decker fishing boat that had been marooned here over twenty years ago. Men and women and a couple of dogs exploring the island. She heard their screams and yelps as one by one the flesh-eating plants and human hybrids attacked their prey, consuming the weakest, keeping only the strongest. Her vision narrowed to a winding jungle path. The elders showed her a sanctuary concealed at the center of the island. *Come into the jungle,* they whispered in her mind. *Surrender...*

Amy's eyes snapped open. The early light of dawn cast the palm trees in silhouette. Panic made her sit up fast. She'd let her guard down. She surveyed the jungle. No sign of Ted. But he'd come in the night. A trail of his footprints dotted the sand from the jungle to where she'd slept. *God, he stood right over me.*

A sudden realization turned her blood cold.

Ted had taken her machete.

She drew her knife and stood. The trees along the beach had gray light between them. Farther back, the jungle was all gloom and clotted foliage.

The yacht's smoldering carcass had cooled. She rubbed the chill bumps on her arms. She was only wearing a T-shirt and bikini underneath. Her windbreaker had been a casualty to the fire. Same with her sandals and the purse that contained her identity. She imagined her face on her passport melting. Her name and address burning to embers. All she had left was her useless, empty flare gun, her knife, and a bag of coconuts.

The fucking bastard's won.

Her eyes watered. Without food, shelter, clothing, her best tool and weapon, how long could she survive?

The sun brightened around the treetops, pushing back shadows in the forest, warming her skin. *Don't give up. There has to be a way.* She picked up one of the gas cans and shook it. There was still fuel at the bottom. She walked around the smoking boat. The fire had burned a couple of trees next to the bow. Their bark still had a few glowing embers. Amy smiled as an idea came to her.

She got everything she needed ready. She thought of Skipper Jim and his daughter, Ellie, living here the past few years as guardians, just as some other man or woman had done before them. *If this island needs a human host to walk out of the jungle, maybe killing Ted, the last guardian, would defeat the island.*

She laughed at the thought as her shaken body filled with courage. She stood where the beach bordered the wall of jungle. "You want me?" she yelled loud enough for the elders to hear. "Then it's either me or Ted! You can't have both!"

All the plants and trees chittered as one living creature. The sound resonated in her bones. Remembering the visions from her dream, she knew where the elders wanted her to go.

29

Amy hiked barefoot through the jungle, holding a burning torch in one hand, the guardian's skull in the other. The necklace with three monkey skulls dangled across her chest. Black ash streaked her forehead and around her eyes like the face paint of Amazonian women she had seen pictured in Boyd's photography books. Amy wore half of a ripped T-shirt over her bikini top. The bottom half of her shirt she had wrapped around the top of a piece of driftwood, saturated the cloth with gasoline, and then made herself this torch.

The moving vines and flesh-eating plants reeled from the fiery end and let her pass. Flowers shrank in her presence. She crossed a freshwater ravine. Weaved through ivy-covered trees, and stepped over logs covered in migrating moss and shuddering mushrooms. She kept her eyes peeled for Ted. She didn't see him anywhere. She could feel his presence though. He taunted her with staccato-fast clicking calls that sounded like they were coming from her left, then her right, then fifty feet ahead.

"Come out and show yourself!" Amy yelled.

The forest went silent. She pictured him crouched, camouflaged against the surrounding plants, the machete in his hand. Every tall bush and massive tree was a place he could jump out from.

Amy moved through the shadowy woods at a cautious pace, whipping her torch from side to side. She came into an area littered with logs. Green skeletal things lay inside the hollow timbers. One of them was barely moving. The skeleton with long black hair might have once been a woman. One of the Filipino castaways? Amy spotted half a dozen others in the logs around her. Those were long dead, their rotten bones melded into the logs. Slower than a sloth, the woman's bony hand with dangled moss reached out of its wooden cocoon toward Amy. She touched her torch to the plants growing around the skeleton. The interior of the log caught fire. The skeletal woman released a weak hiss, then curled up as the flames consumed her.

Amy walked around the edge of the enclosed lagoon filled with stagnant water. The seaweed beneath the surface took interest in her. Stalks poked out of the water, their leafy heads turning as she rounded the lagoon.

The two-story Filipino fishing boat still leaned against the beach. Stepping through a crack, she entered the dark hull. Her firelight lit the way through the cluttered passage. She moved around posts, past a coil of rusty chains. She paused at the metal trunk where they'd found the faded photos of the Filipino crew. She felt confident she had burned the last of them.

It's just me and Ted now.

Again, she sensed him watching her. She looked back toward the crack that led out to the beach. No sign of him. The curious seaweed, too out of reach from their prey, lost interest and sunk beneath the lagoon's surface.

Amy continued to cross through the hull, wary of every dark crevice. She stabbed the torch into the chambers and cargo holds.

Again, she heard rustling up above, followed by the clumps of footsteps.

She froze, heart thumping. She crept with her torch out in front of her. To her left, firelight illuminated the moss-covered stairway that led to the upper deck, where the two-story cabins were located. A face formed in the darkness. The flame flickered in the reflection of a single eye.

Ted grinned. "Hello, sunshine."

Amy halted at the bottom of the stairs. She moved her torch from side to side.

He watched the flame, keeping his distance. "How about you lay down your fire and finally surrender? We'll make this ship our home."

"How about you come down here and let's end this?" she said.

His bony fingers gripped the machete. "You really want to take me on?"

"One of us is going to die today."

"Then come and get me." He dashed off into the darkness, his feet thumping along the upper deck.

Amy started up the stairs. Above her, the upper deck's interior echoed with chitters. Hundreds of purple vines squirmed along the walls, floor, and ceiling. Stalks with pod-shaped heads opened jaws with sticky needle teeth. The vines writhed and snapped at her.

Oh, shit! Amy bolted back down the stairs and through the hull. Her feet slipped in the slimy mulch. Wood cracked behind her where mouths bit into walls. Plants and roots rustled through the deck above her. Stalks slithered out of holes in the ceiling. She burned them with her torch and slapped them away.

Up ahead Ted's bushy form appeared from a second stairway and dashed through a tall, sun-lit hole at the other end of the hull. Amy looked back over her shoulder. A river of purple vines rushed toward her. She ran faster, dodging posts and broken crates. The glowing jagged hole drew closer. Amy burst through the exit and found herself back in the jungle. Her fast-pumping legs carried her twenty yards before stopping. She bent over and sucked in big gulps of air. Sweat dripped off her face. Back at the ship, the vines with gnashing teeth stopped at the hull's broken doorway. A clucking tongue beckoned her to continue into the jungle.

A well-worn path guided her through the trees. At the heart of the island, where it seemed to be darkest, sunlight shined through a narrow gap between the trunks of two wrinkled trees. She crossed through the gap and entered a circular clearing with a dirt floor that stretched twenty feet in diameter.

The sanctuary she'd seen in her dreams.

Six Bodhi trees with wide trunks stood with their roots joined along the ground. Between each tree, gaps led back into the dark jungle. Centered in the sanctuary of trees stood an ancient idol as tall as Amy. Roots grew down the wooden statue's back like a mane of long hair. Thorns covered its body. Amy walked around the idol to the front. Carved into the form of a naked native woman with sharp features, the prickly statue appeared to be some goddess. Her arms were raised to the sky. A necklace with monkey skulls hung across her breasts. Bones were piled around the thorn goddess's feet. Human sacrifices? A thick vine with purple and white flowers had coiled around the broken skeletons and skulls, like a snake protecting its eggs. Its presence here made Amy nervous.

She jabbed her torch at the ivy. It slinked away from the flame and slithered back into the jungle.

To show the elders the enemy warrior they were dealing with, she set the guardian's skull atop the bone pile before their idol. Then she spun in a slow circle holding out the torch, staring down each of the Bodhi trees. "What do you want from me?"

Ted's raspy voice called from the jungle. "Surrender!"

"You know I'll never do that. Not while you're still alive."

She pulled her knife out of its sheath, gripped the torch in her other hand. A stone flew through one of the gaps and struck the idol. It diverted her attention long enough to throw off her guard.

Behind her, Ted howled. His plant-shrouded body charged from between two trees. He wielded the machete over his head. Amy leapt sideways as the blade chopped past her shoulder. Ted's momentum took him to the opposite side of the clearing.

"Forgot how agile you are," he said, grinning.

Shaking with adrenaline, Amy stabbed the air with the torch.

Ted kept his distance from the fire. In the daylight, she saw him for all his hideousness. His twisted, ravaged body had become home to every species of plant on the island. Seaweed hung from his bony limbs. Fungus had collected around the charred hole in his chest where she'd shot him. She could see through the other side. His collapsed, lichen-green face was plated with white mushrooms. The only part of Ted she recognized was the blue eye that gleamed from a socket of his skull.

"It's been fun playing games with you, Amy, but it's time to end this." He wielded the machete and came at her again. She dodged right. His foot kicked her in the side. She fell to the hard ground, losing the torch. He charged toward her. Amy crawled backward until her back bumped into the trunk of a tree.

Ted brought the machete down, burying the blade in the dirt between her legs, narrowly missing her pelvis.

He stood over her. "I couldn't damage that pretty body. Not yet. I've got other things in mind before the jungle takes you." His roving eye moved from her face to her chest. He eased closer, moving his tongue fast. His hand lashed out, ripped her T-shirt.

Amy side-kicked his knee, cracking it at a bad angle.

"Ah, fuck!" Ted collapsed to the ground beside her.

She tried to crawl away. Claws dug into her legs.

Her leg kicked again, caved in his sunken skull even more.

Crying out, he backed away.

Amy stood with her knife held in front of her. Her chest heaved for air.

Laughing, Ted snapped off a couple of his rib bones. A vine shot out. Wrapped around her wrist. Another snatched her ankle. The vines yanked her off her feet. Amy landed hard on her backside. The fall knocked the wind out of her.

The leafy-green ropes pulled her toward Ted's wide spread arms. Carnivorous plants extended their jaws from holes in his ribcage.

With the knife, she sawed the tether around her wrist. The vine broke off. She went for the one around her ankle. Ted lunged into her shoulder. Knocked her on her side. He crawled on his belly, reaching for her. She stabbed his hand. When he withdrew it, she backed up against the wooden idol, felt the prick of its thorns. Ignoring the pain, Amy crouched like a cornered animal, ready to pounce.

On two hands and one knee, Ted crabbed sideways, dragging his broken leg. "You don't play nice. When I finally own that body of yours, I'm not going to play nice either."

"Come any closer," Amy warned, "and I'll break your other leg."

He chuckled. "Won't matter. The island will make me new ones."

Four brown roots grew out of his ribcage and touched the ground on either side of him, giving him an extra set of limbs, like a spider. He scuttled toward her.

Unleashing a cry of rage, Amy leapt and jammed the knife's blade into his eye.

Ted cried out. He pulled at the knife stuck in his skull. Blood and green liquid oozed down his face.

Amy stood and went to the idol's bone pile and picked up the guardian's skull. Tucked inside the brain cavity was Skipper Jim's flask. Her torch still had a small flame on it.

Crawling around the circle, Ted reached blindly for her. "Where are you, bitch?"

She stood behind him and poured a mixture of whiskey and gasoline over his head and shoulders.

"What the hell are you doing?" he yelled.

"You messed with the wrong woman." She touched the torch to his head.

Ted screamed as flames spread down his face and across his shoulders. She tossed more gas-whiskey onto his chest and back. The fire enshrouded him. The carnivorous plants trapped inside his ribcage shrieked. Their jaw-trap heads and stalks curled into ash and embers.

Ted continued to wail.

Amy took her sweet time as she grabbed the machete. She thought of everything this asshole had done to her. Remembered the feeling of that child predator, Boyd, too, stealing her innocence. All Amy's rage unleashed as she brought down the machete and split Ted's burning skull open. The blade dug into a black, spore-covered brain. She kept chopping and chopping until he was nothing but a pile of smoldering broken bones and slimy mush.

Blood and plant matter dripping on her bikini and skin, Amy collapsed on her knees before the thorn goddess statue. Amy shook as adrenaline coursed through her body. Her eyes watered, but she held back any tears. When the shaking stopped, she looked up at the statue's wood-carved face. She placed half of Ted's blackened skull on the pile next to the guardian's.

She felt depleted. Sitting up on her knees, she looked around at the cabal of Bodhi trees. "I'm not going to fight you anymore. Either let me leave this island or kill me now."

Dozens of roots from their trunks stretched across the ground and touched her in reverence. The jungle outside the sanctuary chittered and trees shook their leaves. Green vines snaked through every gap in the trees. Leafy tendrils dotted with flowers gently slid up her body.

Crying and laughing, Amy looked up at the circle of blue sky between the elder's treetops. She held out her arms in surrender as the plants completely covered her.

EPILOGUE

Amy walked through her own private paradise like Eve through Eden. Since she'd become one with the island, her consciousness had connected with all the plants and trees. She communed with every blade of grass and lichen, every fungus and flower. Even the seaweed forest that drifted beneath the surface of the lagoon. As she wandered the jungle, orchids and hanging flowers opened and chirped. The papaya split open to release their purple floating seeds like dandelion. The green-toothed pods crooned to her and parted their vine patches to make her a path. She realized now this island wasn't evil, just doing what it needed to survive in a world overtaken by man.

Her body had wasted away to a skeleton covered in living plant matter. Thorns grew along her arms and legs. All her blood and flesh had been sacrificed to the island. Her corpse thrived on a new life force that mainly required water and sunlight. Like the rest of the plants inhabiting the island, she often craved blood and meat. It was always a treat when the plants caught her a bird. Sometimes the kelp tossed a fish onto the beach.

Amy's exposed skull still had wispy blonde hair that blew in the breeze. A crown of small white flowers grew naturally around her head. Her empty eye sockets were overgrown with lichen, but she could see, thanks to the vision the Bodhi elders had given her. As the last guardian, Amy protected the island, and it looked after her.

The graveyard behind the hut now had four crosses. Amy had buried Skipper Jim's and Ellie's bones next to Gwyn. Sometimes she missed Jasmine and visited her grave. But her memory was fading. Amy could barely remember her face. Since her soul sister had died, Amy had found comfort living as a hermit. As it turned out, being marooned on a deserted island suited her.

Every so often she wandered to the sanctuary, placed an offering of flowers or bird skulls before the idol, and then meditated with the Bodhi trees. Most days, she sat at the entrance of her monkey hut, watching and waiting. The dense border of mangroves shielded the island from the outside world. The lagoon remained closed and hidden. Only when the right prey came along did the mangroves separate to open a channel.

Today a new boat of explorers cruised into the lagoon. Six people onboard.

In the jungle, the plants chittered, eager for a feast. With a primal hunger she shared with the island, Amy grabbed her machete.

ABOUT THE AUTHOR

Brian Moreland writes a blend of mystery, action-adventure, dark suspense and horror. He has written ten books, including *The Devil's Woods, Tomb of Gods, The Witching House, The Seekers, Darkness Rising,* and *Savage Island.* His short stories have appeared in several horror anthologies. His most praised short story is "The Corn Maidens" (in *Midnight in the Pentagram).*

An adventure seeker and world traveler, Brian has visited over twenty countries. He enjoys hiking, caving, and exploring new places. He currently lives in North Texas, where he is creating scary books and short stories.

Website: http://www.brianmoreland.com/
Follow on Twitter: @BrianMoreland
Facebook: https://www.facebook.com/BrianMorelandWriter

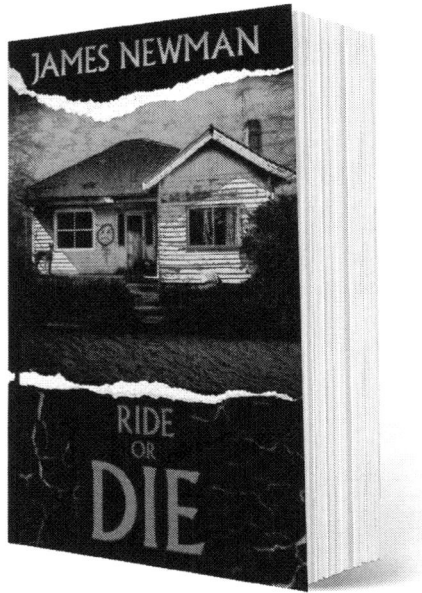

Amelia Fletcher is a good girl. She's a straight-A student, second chair in her middle-school chorus, and she never uses the Lord's name in vain.

But a few days ago, she discovered that her dad has been cheating on her mom.

For the first time in her life, Amelia decides she would like to know what it feels like to be a bad girl. For just one night.

With the help of her BFFs, Cassie and Folline, she plans to teach Dad's "other woman" a lesson. It's harmless fun, right? An evening of teenage mischief. When all is said and done, the homewrecker will go away and never come back. Only then can Amelia's family begin to repair what has been broken.

However, this was no ordinary affair. And the trio could never expect the horrors that await them inside the house on Callaghan Drive.

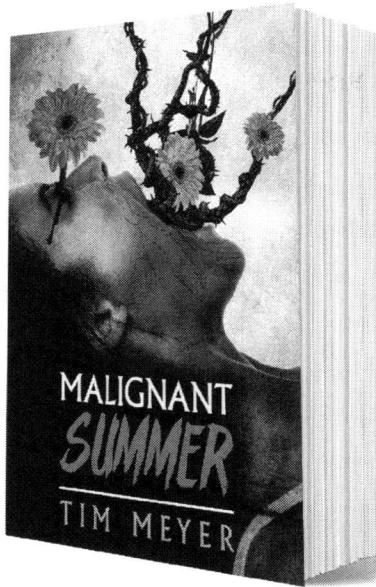

It's 1998 in Hooperstown, New Jersey and people are getting sick. Some citizens blame the local chemical plant. A select few believe something far more terrifying is responsible, a dreadful force that causes nightmarish visions and aberrant illnesses. Bad things are blooming in Hooperstown, and the stench of death is growing stronger...

Standing on the edge of summer break after the longest last day of eighth grade ever, Doug Simms and his two best friends join a group of older kids for an all-night scavenger hunt. It's supposed to be a celebration, an evening of fun and freedom. But what happens that night will change their summer in the darkest ways imaginable. And not just their summer...but their entire lives.

Malignant Summer is a coming-of-age epic where innocence is lost and the path through adolescence is painful. Where dreamscapes merge with reality. Where love seems possible, and the best season feels like it can last forever.

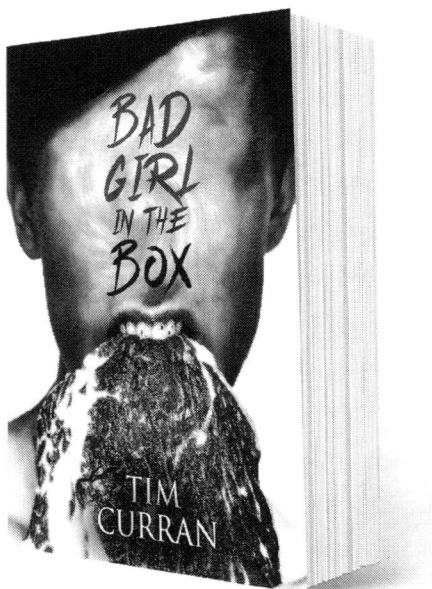

Printed in Great Britain
by Amazon